W9-BFU-233

Some Moves
Are Harder Than Others

So there we were—Lucy on one side of the cafeteria and me on the other. And man, all I wanted to do was dance with her. That's all. Wanted to wrap my arms around her slim waist, pull her close, dance her across that cafeteria floor beneath the cutout stars and paper moons.

And I know for a fact that she wanted to dance with me, too. All I had to do was ask her. Simple, right?

Wrong.

ALL GRADUATING STUDENTS!

Come to the…

Stardust Dance

Friday, May 31

8:00–11:00 P.M.

Dogwood School Cafeteria

Music by the Rot Whilers

Kissing Tennessee

and Other Stories from the Stardust Dance

Kathi Appelt

Harcourt, Inc.

Orlando   Austin   New York   San Diego   Toronto   London

Copyright © 2000 by Kathi Appelt

All rights reserved. No part of this publication may be reproduced
or transmitted in any form or by any means, electronic or mechanical,
including photocopy, recording, or any information storage and retrieval
system, without permission in writing from the publisher.

Requests for permission to make copies of any part
of the work should be mailed to the following address:
Permissions Department, Harcourt, Inc.,
6277 Sea Harbor Drive, Orlando, Florida 32887-6777.

www.HarcourtBooks.com

First Harcourt paperback edition 2004
First published 2000

The Library of Congress has cataloged the hardcover edition as follows:
Appelt, Kathi, 1954–
Kissing Tennessee and other stories from the Stardust Dance/Kathi Appelt.
p.   cm.
Summary: Graduating students relate their stories of
love and heartbreak that have brought them
to their school's magical Stardust Dance.
[1. Schools—Fiction.   2. Interpersonal relations—Fiction.
3. Dance—Fiction.] I. Title.
PZ7.A6455Ki   2000
[Fic]—dc21   99-50505
ISBN 0-15-202249-X   ISBN 0-15-205127-9 (pb)

Text set in Spectrum MT
Designed by Lori McThomas Buley

DOM 10 9 8 7 6 5
4500252044

Printed in the United States of America

R0439968750

For my father, Bill,
who took me down the road to Mandalay

Contents

Invitation

Picture it ...

The tables ... pushed against the walls;
the brown linoleum ... polished;
the air ... wondrous!

At one end a stage—
the drummer came in early,
set up his equipment, and left.
Listen—the cymbals shimmer
soft soft ...

From the ceiling:
paper moons and stars,
Saturn with her rings,
a comet.

On the walls:
all the constellations.

For this one night,
this one room
is no longer the
Dogwood Junior High cafeteria,
not at all.
It's the Stardust Dance.

You're invited.

Dance with Me

Magic happens, see. It's just like on those bumper stickers, the ones that say MIRACLES HAPPEN, or JESUS HAPPENS. I never really took those too seriously. I mean, they're bumper stickers.

Yeah, yeah, I know what you're thinking. *Miracles?* Right. Jesus? Maybe. *But magic?*

I wouldn't have believed it myself before tonight, even though I loved all those fairy tales that my mom used to read to me when I was a little kid.

My favorite was the one about Snow White. Those funky little guys with the beards. The poisonous apple. And that cool mirror the evil stepmother used to talk to. You know, she'd ask it all these questions: *Who's the nicest . . . Who's the sweetest . . . Who's the fairest of them all?* And for a while, everything was hunky-dory.

The mirror always said: *You are, O fair one.* But mirrors never lie, and so one day the mirror told her the truth: *Hey, there's this new girl in town, and sorry, witchie, but she's got the edge in the nice, sweet, and fair categories.*

Of course, it was all make-believe. That's what I thought, anyway. But now I'm telling you, I'm not so sure.

See, there I was at the Stardust Dance.

And there was Lucy White. (Yeah, I know, coincidence.) I swear she was glowing in the candlelight.

The whole cafeteria was full of glitter. The decorations committee had hung these paper moons and cutout stars from the ceiling. All those stars and moons were covered with glitter, and every time the air conditioner blasted them, they spun around and around and glitter drifted down on top of everyone. The glitter and the candles... they made the place look like a fairy castle or something. And right in the middle of the ceiling hung a giant mirror-ball.

Anyway, there was Lucy White. She had on this short white skirt and a blue blouse, and she had her black hair pulled back in this long ponytail that came down to the top of her waist. She had those fairy-tale princesses beat. Even Snow White. I mean, if the witch had popped her question then, Lucy White would have won big time.

So there we were—Lucy on one side of the cafeteria and me on the other. And man, all I wanted to do was dance with her. That's all. Wanted to wrap my arms around her slim waist, pull her close, dance her across that cafeteria floor beneath the stars and moons.

And I know for a fact that she wanted to dance with me, too. All year long I had sat behind her in our first-period English class, watching that black ponytail swish across her back. And every once in a while, her hair would fall onto my desk. I loved to pull it, and when I did, she'd look back at me and smile. Man, that girl can smile. But that was all. She hardly ever said anything. She's the quiet type.

So I was really surprised last week in school when she passed me that note. Me, Tim Hernandez. The note that said, "Ask me to dance. Love, Lucy." I've still got it. In fact, it was tucked into my back pocket during the dance. I could feel its heat through my pants. All I had to do was ask her. Simple, right?

Wrong.

See, this afternoon before the dance, I had stood in front of my bedroom mirror practicing the words: "Dance with me, Lucy." I mean, I wanted to get them right. I even changed clothes and practiced.

First, I tried saying them in my old faded jeans and T-shirt. But I thought the words seemed sort of faded, too. So I put on the black slacks and white oxford shirt I have to wear for choir concerts. But then the words seemed too stiff. So I took those clothes off and threw them on my bed.

I went to my closet to look for something else, but almost all my regular clothes were on the floor in a heap.

Ever since my mom had her "big revelation," I've been doing my own laundry. Man, that was one of the biggest mistakes of my life. One afternoon I was playing this new video game, Blood and Guts. I was controlling Gruesome Gus versus the Crimson Menace, and I had totally waxed the guy. It was this really complex sequence of moves, and I was so excited about conquering the game that I wanted to show it to someone. Unfortunately, the only one home at the time was Mom.

But hey, an audience is an audience, right? So I

dragged her out of the laundry room to witness my dexterity.

"My God!" she exclaimed when Gus decapitated the Crimson Menace and red video-blood coated the screen. "You can do that?"

Uh-oh, I'm thinking, *here it comes.* I was sure, after all that carnage, my mom would banish the game forever. I could almost see the little wheels turning in her head.

But then she said, "If you can do that, I *know* you can operate something as simple as the washer and dryer."

So I've been in charge of my own clothes ever since. Which means, most of the time, my clothes are...Well...see, I figure that whatever's been on the bottom of the heap has had the longest time to air out, so I always try to choose stuff from the bottom. But that was before I got the note from Lucy.

Lucy.

Dark eyes and darker hair. So quiet. So pretty.

Lucy.

She takes up all the space inside me. For the past week I've found myself waiting at corners until she's passed and then I've followed her down the hall.

I've found myself daydreaming about her. I've even found myself sitting beside her at lunch.

Lucy.

Who wrote me a note: "Ask me to dance. Love, Lucy."

So there I was, standing in front of my bedroom mirror in my Fruit Of The Loom underwear, with not one clean shirt. I sniffed my armpits and decided to use both my own Arrid Extra Dry and my dad's Old Spice deodorant for extra protection.

Dad! There was the answer. I'd borrow a shirt from Dad. I didn't think he'd mind. The one I picked out was red-blue-and-green plaid, the one he'd bought from the new Eddie Bauer shop at the Dogwood Mall. Okay, it was a couple of sizes too big. But that just made my shoulders look broader. If I didn't tuck it in, it looked okay. I thought Lucy would like it.

So I looked at myself again in the mirror, with Dad's shirt on, and I thought, *Fine, this is fine.* And I started practicing some more: "Dance with me, Lucy." I tried it with all these expressions. See, my choir teacher, Mrs. Applegate, is always telling us to stand in front of a mirror when we're practicing a song.

"Dance with me, Lucy" isn't exactly a song, but I still wanted to get it just right. First I went "dance-withmelucy," almost in a whisper. But I could hardly hear it myself. Then I tried it with this movie star face. Now, don't get me wrong, I'm no movie star, but I'm not that hard to look at, either.

I kept trying it over and over, probably a hundred times, from a hundred different positions—one foot in front of the other, both feet firmly planted, legs crossed, arms crossed, hands on my hips, hands behind my neck, one hand over my heart. You'd have thought I was auditioning for a play or something.

Well, here's where the magic started up. See, that mirror must've gotten sick and tired of me saying those words, "Dance with me, Lucy," because on about the one-hundred-and-first try, I felt them come flying back at me from the mirror's surface and jam into the back of my throat.

No kidding. I thought I was going to choke. All I could do was stand there, paralyzed. I swear I could hear that stupid mirror laughing. Like maybe it was trying to say, "Hey, Romeo, get a life!"

I turned away from the mirror, sweating from

head to toe. I kept trying to swallow, but I could still feel those words stuck right at the back of my tongue, pushing up against my soft palate. I felt queasy.

When I got downstairs, Mom already had dinner on the table, but I just sort of waved to her. She said something like, "Oh, I guess there'll be refreshments at the dance." I nodded. I was afraid if I opened my mouth, I might lose it all over the kitchen table.

Then I thought, *Geez, I can't go to the dance like this,* but as soon as I thought that, I remembered the note in my back pocket: "Ask me to dance. Love, Lucy." It was the *love* part that got me. "Love, Lucy." I had to go.

So I swallowed hard, and when Dad dropped me off at the school cafeteria, without even once mentioning the fact that I was wearing his new shirt, I thought the words had come unstuck. I was actually all right for a few minutes.

The cafeteria was decorated, the lights were low, the band was already playing. Everything seemed great. Great. Wonderful. But then I saw Lucy.

There she was, standing against the wall on the other side of the room. As soon as I saw her, those stupid words boiled back up, clogging my mouth like the wad of cotton my dentist uses when he fills a cavity. I reached up to wipe my chin, just to make sure I wasn't drooling.

Quickly I found an open spot along the opposite wall, leaned against it, and concentrated hard on not throwing up.

Now here's where I became a real believer in magic. Lucy didn't know I was strangling on those words or that the note in my pocket felt like a branding iron on my rear end. She must've thought I was just being a jerk, ignoring her the way I was. I tried hard not to look at her, but I couldn't help it.

Finally I looked up instead, and right at that instant, the mirror-ball began to spin. Diamonds of light spilled across the room. Now this sounds cuckoo, but I swear, one of those tiny panes of glass caught Lucy's reflection and twirled it around the room—across the metal chairs lined up against the wall, across the crackling ice in the punch bowl, over the acoustic tiles in the ceiling and the waxed vinyl tiles on the floor—until it dashed right across my lower jaw, where it paused for the merest, fleetingest flash of a second, hardly long enough to notice but long enough to sear through the skin and bone. Long enough to send just enough heat to thaw my frozen tongue and melt that clump of words.

That was all it took.

Next thing I knew, Lucy was snuggled up against me, her ponytail falling over the back of my hands, gold and silver glitter in her hair—the fairest of them all.

Yes sir, get me one of those bumper stickers: MAGIC HAPPENS.

Rachel's Sister

Mary Sarah Luther stood in front of a bathroom mirror in Dogwood Junior High School and thought, *Tonight I can be beautiful.* Then she pulled her long brown hair back and began to tie it with a bright red ribbon. Rachel's ribbon.

It was early in the evening, and she could hear the music playing in the cafeteria down the hall, where Sky Williams was leaning against the wall, waiting for her, waiting to take her picture. *My picture,* she thought.

She looked back into the mirror. *I might be beautiful enough to be the Stardust Queen.* The image in the mirror didn't say a word otherwise. Then she thought, *I might be as beautiful as Rachel.*

———

Rachel. Ever since that night two months ago, a Tuesday night, when her sister, Rachel—three years older, with her blue eyes and silky brown hair—came into the bedroom they shared and tossed something onto the bed where Mary Sarah was studying for her history exam, everything had changed.

"Hey!" said Mary Sarah, looking at the short golden fluted tube. When she realized what it was, she recoiled in horror.

"Get it out of here!" she yelled at her sister.

Rachel just stood there, smiling, while Mary Sarah backed away from the tube that rolled toward her on the bed, rolled down the mattress as if it were chasing her.

"You trying to get us killed?" Mary Sarah asked. The golden tube gleamed in the bedroom light and came to rest against a wrinkle on the bedspread. "You know what Daddy'll do if he finds this?"

Rachel put both hands on her hips. "I don't care," she said flatly. "I can wear lipstick if I want. I'm seventeen, for heaven's sake." She said it as if being seventeen made all the difference, as if her age were something that could change the facts of their existence, which included being members of the Holy

Brethren of Jesus Tabernacle Church, where tests of devotion had nothing to do with being seventeen.

"I don't care," Rachel repeated. The possibilities inside those words hovered in the room like a dark bird.

Mary Sarah shuddered.

Rachel was changing. Ever since she had begun to be friendly with Robert Dunn—a big handsome boy in her junior class at Dogwood High School, a boy with sandy hair and brown eyes, who smiled easily—things had been different. At first it was small differences that most people wouldn't even notice.

But Mary Sarah did. She noticed Rachel spent more time in front of their dresser mirror in the morning. She saw Rachel twist her hair into a knot at the back of her neck, hair that, like her own, had not been cut for the past seven years because according to their daddy, cutting it was a sin.

Then one day, while they were riding the bus together, Rachel had pulled out a bright red ribbon from her notebook pocket and tied it around her hair. Mary Sarah had shivered when she saw it. "Rachel," she hissed, "take it off. What if someone tells?"

"Who's going to tell?" Rachel replied, gazing pointedly at Mary Sarah.

Mary Sarah was startled at how pretty her sister looked, the red ribbon peeking out from behind her neck. It seemed to light up her face. Mary Sarah turned her head and stared out the bus window at the pumpkin-colored dirt roads that led to the highway and would eventually take them into Dogwood to school. Their house was set back off the main road, back within the pine forest, just under seven miles from town. There were only a few other families that lived back in there, mostly folks whose children were grown.

Until Mary Sarah and Rachel were old enough to attend school in town, they'd had only each other for playmates, and the three years that Rachel went to school before Mary Sarah was old enough to go, too, were the three longest years of Mary Sarah's life. Right after lunch on school days, she'd walk to the end of the drive and wait the two hours until the bus stopped and Rachel was released into her waiting arms. The only exceptions had been the days her mother took Mary Sarah into town to visit Grandmother Lacey.

Mary Sarah wished they could visit Grandmother Lacey more often. She loved her grandmother's rambling old house, right next to the high school, where she had taught English for more than twenty years. But Daddy wouldn't allow it. "The woman's too much in the world," he'd tell her mother. "It's bad enough they make us send the girls to school." Then he'd look at his oldest daughter. "There's wickedness out there."

Sometimes Rachel would lower her eyes and whisper, "Amen."

Rachel was pretty. Like their mother, Charlene. There was no denying that. Her family, the people at the Holy Brethren of Jesus Tabernacle, friends at school—all of them said, "Rachel is so pretty. Such a pretty face." Then they would look at Mary Sarah, her face down. "Why, you're pretty, too, Mary Sarah," they'd say. But Mary Sarah didn't believe them. She knew she was plain.

She was Mary Sarah of the plain brown hair and plain brown eyes. Mary Sarah of the shadows, along the edges of sight.

As the bus pulled to a stop at the high school, Mary Sarah watched her sister bounce down the steps, smiling, the ribbon glowing. There was Robert Dunn, smiling, too, while Rachel walked over to him. Mary Sarah watched through the window of the bus as Robert gently took her sister's hand and walked with her toward the school. She saw Rachel turn her head and smile up at him. The morning sun seemed to wrap itself around the two, wrap them into a ball of gold.

It was lovely, watching them. Rachel so happy. Robert so gentle. Mary Sarah kept that image of the two of them in her mind all the way to her own school, Dogwood Junior High.

After the red ribbon, there were other things about Rachel that changed. For instance, she began to wear jewelry. First a small gold chain around her neck, then a bracelet. Mary Sarah thought Rachel carried herself differently, too—held her shoulders back, stood up a little straighter.

Of course, Rachel took off all those "adornments" before she got home. Mary Sarah watched her sister untie her red ribbon from around her hair and carefully tuck it, along with the chain and bracelet, back into the pocket of her binder while they rode home on the bus. Times like this, when Mary Sarah felt

her own longings for adornments such as these stir inside her, she thought, *We must be evil.*

Except on that night two months ago, as she'd looked at her sister standing by the mirror with her lipstick on, Mary Sarah hadn't seen an evil person at all. She just saw her seventeen-year-old sister, Rachel, the same sister who helped her with her homework, who took good care of all her clothes because she knew they'd be passed down to her, who, when they had both been small, sang to her on scary nights after the lights were turned off.

She's the one who hugged me and hugged me, thought Mary Sarah, remembering the long-ago day Daddy lifted her off the ground and pulled down her cotton shorts right in the front yard and spanked her with his broad leather belt, spanked her so hard that welts rose up on the backs of her thighs, spanked her for riding too close to his new Ford pickup truck on her bicycle and scratching the green paint with her handlebars, and then spanked her again for wetting herself after he was done. Mary Sarah was only seven when it happened. Rachel was ten.

Mary Sarah remembered seeing Mama's face,

watching through the kitchen window, frozen. It was Rachel who'd yelled, "Stop it, Daddy!" and pulled at his strong arms until he shoved both of the girls away. It was Rachel who'd helped her put her shorts back on, taken her to their room, and lain down beside her until she'd stopped sobbing. Mary Sarah remembered feeling Rachel's heart beating against her back and hearing her sing "This Old Man" softly, over and over in her ear.

That was right before Daddy heard "the word of the Lord" in his own ear from the bottom of his bottle of Gilbey's Gin, saying, "Rise up, Thomas Luther. Rise up and take your rightful place." Ever since then, seven years before, he hadn't touched a drop of gin or either one of the girls. But that didn't mean he wouldn't.

And if he saw Rachel with these adornments... Mary Sarah felt the fine hairs on her freckled arms stand up.

Daddy was late that night two months ago, as he was most nights since the Lord had spoken to him. He witnessed for Christ with several other men from the lumber mill where he worked pushing logs from the flatbed trailers of timber trucks onto conveyor belts. Right after work they met at the Holy Brethren of Jesus Tabernacle and prayed for direction from God.

Mama always made Mary Sarah and Rachel wait until he got home to eat, no matter how late it was. The smell of dinner—pork chops with brown gravy, panfried corn bread, and cooked okra with fresh tomatoes—hovered in the still air. Mary Sarah's stomach growled. It was already after nine o'clock.

She listened for the familiar rumble of the pickup, with the telltale sound of the tailgate banging up and down. The latch had broken several years before, and rather than repair it, Daddy just let it rattle, no longer concerned about the truck's appearance. The loud bang the tailgate made when he drove over the dip at the end of the drive was the signal that he was home.

Despite the growing emptiness she felt in her stomach, Mary Sarah silently prayed that Daddy would be extra late. Outside their small frame house, the spring air was as damp as the wet orange clay that clung to Daddy's Red Wing boots.

Mary Sarah knew he'd be home any minute, and as soon as he stepped outside the truck, he'd stop at the shed beside the drive. There he'd take his rag, tip the can of kerosene onto it, and rub it over his arms to remove the sticky pine resin that had splattered on him during the day at the mill. Once he'd wiped it off, he'd hold his arms under the faucet next to the house. But he still always smelled like kerosene.

"I'll take the smell of kerosene over liquor anytime," Mama said. Mary Sarah agreed.

Her mother was a petite woman, small boned and delicate. She reminded Mary Sarah of the tiny vireos, the gray birds that lined the electric cable running from the utility pole beside the road to their house. At fourteen Mary Sarah was already taller than Mama by a head. In fact, she was already taller than Rachel, too, who was built more like their mother.

Rachel. Mary Sarah shuddered as she sat on her bed and heard her sister repeat those words, "I don't care," her lips coated with the deep, creamy red Revlon Pearls of Passion that had come from the small golden tube shimmering on top of the bedspread.

Mary Sarah looked up at her. Rachel's face seemed to glow. It was a beautiful face, rosy and radiant.

Suddenly Mary Sarah realized something. Rachel

looked exactly like the photograph at Grandmother Lacey's house of their mother on her wedding day. Smiling, sweet, aglow. "Doesn't Mama look like a queen in that picture?"

Mary Sarah always agreed. She loved the photograph—the soft blush of their mother's cheeks, the strand of pearls around her throat, the veil of lace that swept across her shoulders.

It was almost nine-thirty. Mary Sarah heard the bang of the tailgate. A little while later she heard her mother call, "Come to dinner. Daddy's home." From the other room the screen door slammed. Mary Sarah looked up at Rachel. Her sister's face had turned white.

"Rachel, take it off," Mary Sarah whispered.

"No...I...," Rachel stammered. Then she looked at Mary Sarah, her resolve slipping away. "Run to the bathroom and grab the Vaseline..." But before Mary Sarah could budge from her bed, she heard Daddy's footsteps coming down the short hallway. "What's taking you girls so long? Didn't you hear your mother?"

Then there was the turning of their doorknob,

and bits of Daddy began to slip through — first his hand, then his arm, then the word "Dinner," followed by his mouth, his nose, and finally his eyes, eyes that narrowed sharply when he saw his oldest daughter's painted lips.

"Why, you little *jezebel*!" He spit the word as if it were poison. Mary Sarah couldn't take her eyes off his. Only a few weeks before, Brother Jepson had caught a rare bobcat in one of his fox traps and invited them to come see it. She remembered the cat, tethered to a sycamore tree in the preacher's backyard, its front paw almost completely severed, dangling at the end of its leg.

"Reckon we're a lot like this bobcat," Brother Jepson had remarked to Daddy. "Not too many of us true believers left."

"Amen, brother," Daddy had replied.

The cat had pulled its ears back almost flat against its head and hissed, baring its dangerous teeth — its eyes burning.

They had shaken Mary Sarah to her very core, those eyes. And here they were again. Only now they were her father's.

Daddy grabbed Rachel by her hair and pulled her from the room. Mary Sarah jumped from her bed to follow them. She tried to scream, "Stop it, Daddy!" just as Rachel had done for her all those years ago, but the words wouldn't come.

And Rachel? Rachel didn't say anything. Daddy dragged her into the living room and threw her against the sofa. He turned to Mama. "Get a wash-cloth, Charlene!" She hurried to the bathroom and returned with a pale green cloth. She held it out toward him. He snatched it from her hand and stormed out the front door.

The room blazed with light from the two lamps beside the sofa. Rachel sat there on the cushions. Her eyes were shut. Her hands were folded in front of her. Mary Sarah stared. Was Rachel shrinking?

She was praying. Shrinking and praying. Her voice a whisper, "Have mercy on me, Jesus. Have mercy." Mama stepped back into the kitchen, disappeared. Even though Mary Sarah couldn't see, she was almost certain Mama was standing in front of the window, looking out into the dark night.

Daddy threw open the door, his bobcat eyes furious. An overpowering smell of kerosene exploded into the room. Mary Sarah's eyes began to burn. She again tried to scream, but still no words came out. Daddy grabbed Rachel's hair and yanked her to her feet.

"You'd better keep praying, sister!" Daddy shouted.

Mary Sarah could hear Brother Jepson's words from church pounding in her ears. "Turn your backs, brothers and sisters! Shun the many adornments of the world that lead only to evil!" And Daddy shouting, "Amen, brother! Tell it like it is!"

Mary Sarah shook her head. Daddy's lips curled into a snarl. "No jezebel is going to darken the rooms of this house!" Then Mary Sarah saw him pull Rachel's head back and wipe her mouth with the cloth. "You understand?" he yelled.

Rachel twisted against Daddy. She tried to push him away with both of her hands, but he yanked her head back farther and continued to rub her mouth with the rough kerosene-soaked cloth.

Mary Sarah saw the green cloth begin to turn bright red. She saw a thin line of blood run down the back of Daddy's hand. It was coming from Rachel's nose.

Rachel continued to twist against him. Her eyes were shut tight. Mary Sarah shut her own eyes. She could hear a roaring sound in her ears, like the wind when it rushes through the upper stories of the pines during a storm. Where was it coming from? There was no wind in the room. She opened her eyes and looked at Rachel. Her chest heaved as she twisted against Daddy. He seemed to be rubbing harder. Spit was coming out the right side of his mouth. His eyes narrowed. Suddenly Rachel stopped twisting, her body slumped, her knees buckled.

Daddy held her up by the chin and then lifted her in one swift motion and, as hard as he could, slammed her down toward the floor.

Mary Sarah heard a sickening *whack* as Rachel's face hit the side of the wooden coffee table before she landed on the braided rug. The roaring in Mary Sarah's ears screeched to a stop. Daddy balled the cloth in his fist, threw it as hard as he could, and stormed out the front door. Like a bright red butterfly flying into glass, the cloth hit the wall, unfurled, and silently slipped to the floor.

From the corner of her eye, Mary Sarah saw a flurry of movement and heard Mama run through the door behind Daddy. She could hear the engine of the pickup begin to turn over, and then above the rattle, she heard her mother's voice shout, "No, Thomas, no! Don't go!" Mary Sarah waited to hear the grinding of the gears as he shifted into reverse, but the sound didn't come.

She looked down. Rachel wasn't moving. A pool

of blood was forming on the rug, seeping into the beige and blue and copper-colored threads.

As if she were being propelled by an outside force, Mary Sarah began to shake her sister. At last her throat relaxed and allowed her voice to come. "Please, Rachel, please wake up!"

Rachel just lay there, her breath coming in shallow wisps. Mary Sarah grabbed a dish towel from the kitchen and began to mop the blood that continued to seep from her sister's nose. Then she placed the towel beneath Rachel's face and went to get a wet cloth. Maybe the coolness would wake her. Mary Sarah had to get her sister off the floor and into the safety of their bedroom. Once there she'd lock the door, she'd push her bed against it, she'd fasten the window. She'd keep Rachel out of Daddy's sight.

"Wake up, Rachel!" she begged.

But Rachel wasn't moving. Kerosene fumes filled the room.

Mary Sarah could hear her mother, outside, pleading with her father. "We'll do better, Thomas, you'll see." The Ford's engine continued to rattle.

Mary Sarah began to wipe Rachel's face. The face that until just a few moments ago had been so beautiful was beginning to swell. As Mary Sarah gently wiped she noticed that her sister's lips were split in a dozen places. Then Mary Sarah gasped. One split ran from the top of Rachel's upper lip to the bottom of her nose. Blood was running from the ragged cut.

A wave of nausea rose in Mary Sarah and she clenched her teeth.

"Wake up, Rachel!" she cried. She had to do something right away. She began to shake her sister hard. "Wake up!" The Ford's engine stopped. Any minute Daddy and Mama would be back inside, and she must have her sister out of sight.

"Please, please wake up!" The cloth in her hand had turned red, just like the one her father had used. Mary Sarah clenched it in her fist. If only she could make Rachel invisible. Mary Sarah thought about all the prayers she had been forced to learn over the past seven years—prayers of thanksgiving, prayers for people in the hospital, prayers of forgiveness—but not one of them was a prayer for invisibility. Not one.

"Rachel!" she sobbed. Then for no other reason than there was nothing else she knew to do, Mary Sarah lay down against her beautiful sister, wrapped her arms around her quiet body, pressed her heart as closely to her sister's as she could, and began to sing.

Sometime later Mary Sarah woke up, still dressed in her school clothes, stiff from lying in one position on the hard floor. The house was dark and quiet. Every light was off. In her hand she felt the moist cloth she had used to wipe Rachel's face.

Rachel! Mary Sarah reached over. Her sister wasn't there. She started to speak, but before she could say anything, she felt a finger on her mouth.

"Shh . . . ," she heard. Then Rachel took her hand and pulled her to her feet. Quietly Rachel led them to the front door, twisted the latch, and turned the knob.

It was lighter outside than it had been in the house. Mary Sarah could see the sharp edges of the pine trees lining their drive. They passed the Ford, with its broken tailgate.

Rachel pulled her along. "Let's go!" Mary Sarah was glad she couldn't see her sister's face. Quickly they walked the seven miles toward town, toward their grandmother's house.

———

That had been two months ago. Rachel's face was almost completely healed. The scar would always be there, though her grandmother told her it would fade with time. And maybe she'd even be able to have plastic surgery to repair it. But Rachel said she liked it. "It makes me feel brave, Grandma," she said, holding her shoulders back.

Rachel is brave, thought Mary Sarah. It was Rachel who had led them all the way to Grandmother Lacey's house through the darkness. Rachel who didn't even blink as she sat in the Dogwood County Hospital emergency room while a young doctor stitched up her lip. Rachel who refused to say anything to the policeman who came to question her.

No, Rachel wouldn't say anything to the policeman. But she said something to Mary Sarah. Something about Mama and Daddy: "We're dead to them."

Once she said it, Mary Sarah knew she was right. There were no telephone calls, no letters, no sign that their parents even realized they were gone.

But Mary Sarah knew that she and Rachel weren't dead. She had watched as the gash on Rachel's lip healed, bit by bit.

Robert Dunn didn't seem to mind the cut. He still held Rachel's hand whenever he came by after school. Because Grandmother Lacey lived in town, the girls no longer had to ride the bus.

Grandmother Lacey bought Rachel hair ribbons in every color. "A girl needs to look pretty once in a while." She smiled, then glanced at the wedding picture of her daughter.

It *was* a pretty picture.

And now, tonight, here was Mary Sarah tying a ribbon around her own hair, as she stood in front of the bathroom mirror at the Stardust Dance. A red one.

Then she pulled a small golden tube out of her purse and held it out in front of her. It glimmered, sparkled in the fluorescent light, caressed the palm of her hand.

Just a Kiss, Annie P.

You! Annie Price Jackson. See me now? Right here in the middle of the Stardust Dance, right here on the dance floor with Brooke Patterson? You're not the only one with blue eyes. No, Brooke's got blue eyes, too. Looking right at me. See?

Do you see, Annie Price Jackson?

Maybe this is the way it should be, huh? Maybe this is better? Maybe Brooke will be the Stardust Queen. And I might be the King. Hey, you never know.

You hear that song the band just played? They sang that one line over and over: *"Look at me now. . . . I'll show you how . . . I'm doing just fine without you."*

That's the way it is, girl. Brooke's eyes. Just as blue as yours. Blue like the sky, like the sea, like something you could fall into and then sink right to the bottom of.

After you left I sank, that's for sure, sank like a stone in water.

Look at me now. . . .

I'm all dried off now, Annie Price Jackson. Dry as a bone. Dry as the Mojave in the summer. Except sometimes, like now, I still wish it was you I was looking at, face-to-face.

Like that night at the Dogwood County Fair last fall. I didn't mean to get hooked up with you. I mean, I knew who you were and you knew who I was. After all, we were on the eighth-grade track team together. Seemed like every time I saw you up until that night, you were running.

You were even running in that picture of you that they had in the paper. The one where you'd won the Piney Woods Cross-Country Invitational. You were running.

But you weren't running at the fair. No, you were taking a turn at the shooting gallery. I was walking by with my buddy Sam Edmundson, and I just happened to look over. You were standing there in your black Doc Martens boots, with this short shimmery blue dress, both of your elbows raised, your cheek resting against the stock of the air rifle.

You were staring so hard at that metal duck that everyone around you stopped. Even me. Even Sam. Even the man behind the counter, with his greasy mustache and red nose. It was like we had to, *had* to stop—stop walking, stop laughing, stop breathing—like everything was so frozen that even the dust stood right where it was in the carnival air, until you finally pulled that trigger.

Kapow! That duck was a goner. Then you burst into a laugh as big as a hot-air balloon, and just like Annie Oakley, you lowered the rifle and blew across the top of it. That's when you looked right at me, looked at me over the top of that gun while the man handed you a pink stuffed tiger, which you tucked underneath your arm without even nodding to him.

The whole time you never stopped looking at me. And I never stopped looking at you. I was afraid to stop, afraid you might turn away.

And while I kept looking right at you, out of the corner of my mouth I told Sam, "Quick, lend me a dollar!" Sam didn't even hesitate; he just reached into his jeans pocket, pulled out a crumpled bill, and stuffed it into my palm.

"Two!" I said to the carny. He slipped me two tokens, and I reached over and gave one to you, Annie Price Jackson. You smiled. "Oh, you think you can beat me, huh?" You still never stopped looking at me.

"No," I said, and handed you the other token, "I just want to see you do that again."

"Nah," you said, laying the air rifle on the red-topped counter and shoving the pink tiger over to me. It was soft in my hands. I wanted to look down at it, but I couldn't. Then you took the tokens and walked away, brushing your wavy brown hair over your shoulder, hair that always seemed to be flying, even in the calmest air.

You looked over your shoulder. "C'mon," you said. But I was stuck. My feet were nailed to the ground. Then Sam gave me a shove and said, "See ya, buddy," and walked away in the other direction.

"C'mon," you said again, laughing. I must have looked ridiculous standing there, not able to get my feet to budge even though I was wearing Nikes, which if you believe the ads should have let me "Just do it." Not these Nikes. They were just sticking to it.

And so was I. With a pink stuffed tiger in my hands. And you calling.

Calling me. "Russ—Russ Mills!" Then you started walking backward. I guess when you said my name, you broke the frozen-feet spell, 'cause suddenly they let go.

Next thing I knew, you were giving my... Sam's... tokens to the guy at the Ferris wheel. One for you and one for me. I wanted to tell you that I hate Ferris wheels. That once when I was real little, my mother made my big sister, Nan, take me on the Ferris wheel. I guess riding the Ferris wheel with her little brother was the last thing she wanted to do. When it stopped at the top, she said, "Look down there, Russ," pointing to the ground a million miles away. "See that clear spot where there aren't any people standing?" I looked, but it seemed like there were people everywhere.

"See it?" she said. I shook my head. "Right down below us, right by the fence."

I looked again. There was a little bit of space. "I see it," I told her.

"Good." She laughed. "That's where I'm going to pitch you out."

Almost as soon as she said it, the carny tripped

the brake and the Ferris wheel lunged forward. My little bottom lifted right out of the seat. It was only an inch or two, but it felt like I was shooting toward that empty space, with no one to catch me. I started screaming, screaming so loud I couldn't even hear Nan's shouts. "I was just kidding!" she shouted. But the only thing I heard was my own screams. Nan said I kept screaming for at least twenty minutes after we got off the Ferris wheel, until Mama finally bought me a big cotton candy to get me to shut up. Nan had to pay for it out of her own money.

So there you were, another girl, luring me onto the Ferris wheel. Should I just start screaming right away and get it over with? But you were saying, "Russ, c'mon, we can see the stars from up there," and you pointed straight up. I couldn't see any stars. The midway lights were too bright.

But I could see you, Annie Price Jackson. You in your shimmery blue dress and eyes to match. You with your wavy brown hair and your straight white teeth. I could see you.

Look at me now. . . . I'll show you how . . .

And what do you know, the stars did come out.

———

So look, Annie Price Jackson, the cafeteria here at Dogwood Junior High is filled with stars, too. Brooke helped with the decorations. She painted comets and stars and planets all around the room, painted them on blue paper, blue like her eyes, see?

Brooke's really great at art. And that's not all she's great at. Like now, you can see her dance. She's been taking dance lessons since she was three years old, and she moves like she doesn't have any bones in her whole body. So, look at us together, Brooke and me. Right here at the Stardust Dance, surrounded by comets. I want to kiss her.

I've never kissed Brooke. I've only kissed you. You're the only girl I've ever kissed.

It was funny the way it happened. There we were at your house on Christmas Day, sitting in the kitchen. Your mother had just made hot chocolate. She was telling us about something she had done one Christmas when she was a girl, but neither of us was listening. You know why we weren't listening. Because when you had asked me what I wanted for Christmas, I'd said, "Just a kiss, Annie P."

So that kiss-not-given was there in the kitchen with you and your mother and me. It was blocking out the sound of the football game piping in from the den, where your father sat in his La-Z-Boy. It was blocking out your little brothers, Matt and Troy, who were arguing over a new game they had gotten for their PlayStation. That kiss-not-given was so strong it was blocking out every word in the universe—all sounds, all noises.

Then your mother finished telling her story. We could see her lips stop moving. She wiped off the counter where the hot chocolate had splashed, dropped the sponge into the sink, and walked into the den to watch the football game with your father. Who was playing? The Saints and the Patriots? Maybe it was the Cowboys and the Giants. I don't know.

As soon as your mother left, I moved toward you. The closer I came, the more I noticed the smells in the room, on you, around us—chocolate, vinyl, dishwashing soap, Gleem toothpaste, rosemary... sweat, which was breaking out all over me.

You just burst out laughing. I wanted to sink into the floor, but your laughing made *me* laugh. We laughed so hard, tears were falling into our hot chocolate. Then you stood up and said, "C'mon, let's go for a run." That's you, Annie P., always running. I got better at running, from being with you. We ran all over Dogwood County. Through Pinewood Forest, our subdivision. Across the dam by Bear Cove Reservoir. Around the Dogwood High School track.

So Christmas Day we ran to the edge of Pinewood Forest, to a vacant field. You stopped and took my hand. The street behind us was empty. Everyone was indoors, either eating or watching the football game or playing with new toys or taking a nap. Only the two of us were out there.

We walked right to the middle of that field where you pulled me down into the brown grass. The day was cold and our breath turned to steam. The ground was hard, but you pulled me down anyway, right down next to you until we were lying in that dry grass and you stretched your body along mine and rolled over on top of me.

What a kiss.

When I said good-bye to you that night, I ran all the way home. I swear the stars were smiling as much as I was. It was such a great kiss, Annie Price Jackson. That night I dreamed of kissing you again. Kissing you on Ferris wheels and kissing you at Dogwood Junior High School between classes, kissing you in your mother's kitchen, kissing you in a field of brown grass. Kissing you every day.

That was the plan I had. But you had another plan, didn't you, Annie P.? The next morning you left early for your run, before the sun even came up. I can see you — blue sweats, your new Avia running shoes that your mom gave you the day before, brown hair flying. I can see you out there, racing along the road to the high school. I can see you, Annie Price Jackson.

But that guy just getting off work at the lumber mill, he couldn't. When he looked down to change the station on his radio, he couldn't see you flying along the shoulder of the road, flying through the air when he hit you. He never saw you.

And neither did I. Never saw you again. Never will see you again.

But look at me now, Annie P.

I'll show you how . . . I'm doing just fine without you.

Starbears

There are few spaces in these east Texas piney woods where the sky is visible in large chunks, where the pine trees stand back enough to allow a wide expanse of clouds and stars to peek through.

The roof of the Dogwood Junior High cafeteria is such a place.

All the graduating eighth graders in Dogwood are packed into the cafeteria below, dancing to the rhythms of the Rot Whilers.

All the eighth graders but one.

This one, Cub Tanner, a tall, lanky boy, almost fifteen years old—in baggy Levi's and a white T-shirt with HAP'S GEE-RODGE written across it in red letters and an old, drab green army shirt over it—this one is not in the cafeteria dancing.

This one is on top of the flat tar roof. With The Question.

He's been here before.

It was a night not long ago—about two weeks, to be exact—a hot humid night similar to this one. His parents and his little brother were all asleep. He could hear his father's faint snoring from down the hall. Cub looked at the clock beside his bed. The green digital numbers read 1:02. He had overslept, and so he had to hurry.

Quickly Cub pulled on his jeans and slipped into his father's old army shirt, faded green with the name TANNER stamped onto a strip of beige webbing above the left pocket. Cub had rescued the shirt from a box of clothing his mother had set aside to give to the Star of Hope Mission. Even though the shirt had been through countless washings since then, it still smelled like his dad.

Cub wouldn't admit it, but when he wore the shirt with his father's smell, it seemed like it was hugging him, like his father used to do when Cub had been small. Back then it seemed as if his father hugged him all the time. But somehow over the years, without

Cub really noticing it, his father had substituted pats on the back, a rub on the shoulder, an occasional tousle of the hair for the great hugs he used to give. Cub didn't want to admit it, but he missed them.

Not only that, but it seemed like his father was always on his case these days, always badgering him about something—grades, homework, his chores. They hardly ever had a conversation anymore that didn't turn into an argument.

Then last year Cub had found the shirt.

It wasn't the same as his father's arms, but wearing it made him feel wrapped in them nonetheless. And he wished like anything that the shirt could answer The Question.

It was not the run-of-the-mill everyday sort of question that popped into your mind, say, when you were studying Spanish or math or some other subject. It wasn't even a specific question. It was more like a bunch of questions all wrapped into a big one: How did he feel about girls? How did they feel about him? How was he supposed to act around them? Was their skin different from his? And there were others he was more afraid to ask, like why did he feel something like a bolt of lightning run up his arm whenever one of his friends—say, Mason or Russ or Sam—shook his hand? Or why couldn't he look into their eyes when they were joking around in the locker room after P.E.? Or how come he felt startled whenever one of the guys slapped him on his butt during a game of tag football? These were all too unsettling to try to answer, so he'd wrapped them into one big thing: The Question.

It sat on Cub's shoulder like a hawk, screeching into his ear, and every so often Cub could feel its invisible talons digging into his shoulder. It clung to him and made him feel uneasy. Not like the comfortable shirt.

But the shirt couldn't help with The Question. It could only hug him. So he wore it every day.

And besides, Trent liked the shirt, too.

"Cool shirt, man," Trent had told Cub the first day he'd worn it to school. The Question had gotten louder since Trent Davis had arrived at Dogwood Junior High.

Cub's plan that night two weeks ago was to meet Trent at school at 1:00 A.M., slip down the street together to Elizabeth Bryan's house, and wrap the bushes in her front yard with toilet paper. Then they would hurry next door to Shannon Perez's house and do the same to her front yard.

The air outside was thick with moisture, dark, and pungent with the smell of wet pine needles. Cub felt his way along the side of his house until he reached the front lawn, where the street lamp offered some visibility.

He grabbed his skateboard from the porch and walked quickly to the street, slick from the dew that clung to the pines, the saint augustine grass, the Ford pickups, the Chevrolet minivans that lined the curbs. He set the board on the concrete and pushed off into the night.

The sound of his skateboard's wheels on the damp pavement boomed in the quiet. What if he woke up the neighbors as he rolled down the street? Cub stepped off quickly. He looked over his left shoulder, expecting to see the lights in the houses flick on one by one. But nothing happened, so he put his board back down and pushed off again.

Soon he found himself moving toward brighter and brighter lights, his green army shirt flapping wildly as he careered forward, like a moth, zooming toward the lights of Dogwood. His heart was racing. *Trent had better be there,* he thought, as he rolled out of his dark neighborhood.

Cub had never met anyone like Trent Davis. Trent had moved to Dogwood all the way from Chicago right after spring break, in mid-March. He was tall, like Cub, five-foot-ten or -eleven, and lanky, too. But unlike Cub, with his shaggy brown hair, Trent had curly black hair, cut short and neat.

Also unlike Cub, who was fairly quiet and kept mostly to himself, Trent was loud and outgoing, full of jokes that he told in his warm midwestern accent. It seemed to Cub that Trent was always smiling or laughing. Add to that his natural ability in sports, and it wasn't long before Trent Davis was one of the most popular boys at Dogwood Junior High.

Especially with the girls, thought Cub. Particularly one.

From the back of their Pre-Algebra class that spring, Cub saw Elizabeth Bryan slip notes to Trent almost every day. Cub saw how Trent would smile whenever he opened a note and then write something at the bottom of the page, fold it up, and slip it

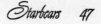

back to her. He saw how Elizabeth blushed when she read what he'd written.

As Cub watched the two of them pass their notes back and forth, he wished he had someone to exchange notes with. He looked across the room at Nancy Sawyer, with her red hair and freckles. Nancy always had a smile. And there was Nancy's best friend, Kelly Watson, who never failed to score higher than everyone else by at least ten points on their Pre-Algebra exams and whose blue eyes reminded Cub of the morning glories his mother grew beside their back steps.

Then there was Shannon Perez, dark and slender, athletic, a champion on the girls' basketball team. Shannon's locker was right next to Cub's, and sometimes she bumped into him while they were standing there, lockers open. She'd start laughing, grab his elbow for a moment, and then wave good-bye.

Maybe Cub could exchange notes with her? He reached into his binder for a sheet of paper. "Dear Shannon," he wrote on the top line. He paused to consider what to say next, when suddenly Trent Davis knocked on Cub's desk with his knuckles. Cub looked up. Trent's intense expression startled him.

Cub felt his hand freeze above the lined paper, and he quickly covered the "Dear Shannon" part with his other hand. There was a moment of silence, then Trent said, "Hey, I hear you're the master of skateboarding around here."

It was true. Cub knew all the best routes in town. The ones with good slopes and smooth curbs. The ones without loose dogs that ran after you as you rolled along. The ones where there was little traffic.

"Want to show me around?" Trent asked. And before he knew it, Cub found himself saying yes. He shoved the paper into his binder. *Another day,* he thought, as he watched Shannon walk out of the room with the other girls, her laughter floating down the hall after her.

That afternoon he'd met Trent at the park on the corner of Landon and Birch. There they'd practiced ollies and kickflips, frontside and backside grinds. Cub was impressed with Trent's ability with a skateboard. Until then Cub had been the only serious skater in town, and because there wasn't anyone else to skate with, he had spent plenty of time cruising the streets and sidewalks of Dogwood alone.

Being there at the park with Trent that day, the

spring sun slipping through the pine trees, the air unusually cool for that late in the season, made him realize how glad he was to have someone to be with. He felt lucky.

Luck reminded him of Moon Pies.

Cub couldn't believe Trent had never tasted one.

"They don't have 'em in Chicago!" Trent had told him that afternoon as they sat eating them on the steps at Hap's Gee-Rodge, the combination auto repair shop and minimarket at the corner of Simms and East Bayou.

That sure gave Cub a new appreciation for Dogwood, Texas. Moon Pies had been Cub's favorite junk food for as long as he could remember, at least since the time years ago when he and his father had gone fishing at Lake Livingston and hadn't caught anything all day. In frustration his father had broken off a piece of a Moon Pie and slipped it onto his hook. To Cub's surprise a largemouth bass swam by and swallowed that chunk of Moon Pie and his father's hook as well.

That evening they'd had fried bass for dinner and leftover Moon Pie for dessert. After that Cub always thought of Moon Pies as lucky.

Trent put the last piece of pie in his mouth and smiled. "Cub Tanner's Good Luck Moon Pies." He laughed. He wiped his hands on his jeans. "Got any more change? I want to buy another one."

Cub dug down into his pocket and pulled up a quarter, two dimes, a couple of nickels, and some pennies. He handed it all to Trent, who went inside and came back with a cellophane-wrapped pie sticking out of his shirt pocket. "I'll bet Elizabeth loves these, too," he said, patting the pocket and looking directly at Cub. "Maybe if I give her one of these, I'll get lucky."

"Yeah, right," Cub said. But he wondered what Trent meant by "lucky"? Did he mean holding hands, kissing, maybe reaching underneath her blouse . . . ?

"Hey!" Trent's voice interrupted Cub's thoughts. "Maybe you oughta buy one for Shannon. Maybe you could catch *her*, too."

Cub's mouth dropped open. "How did . . . ?" Then he remembered the note he had been writing. Trent must have seen it. He felt his cheeks heating up. He looked over at Trent, who was standing there trying to hold in his laughter, but it was no use. The laughter just burst out of him.

Suddenly Cub's embarrassment turned into a vision of Shannon as a mermaid, swimming toward a Moon Pie on a fishing hook. It startled him. Soon laughter grabbed Cub, too, and rolled over him in waves. He kept trying to get ahold of himself, but then he'd look over at Trent and burst into laughter again.

Finally, Hap himself walked over and politely asked them to clear out.

Cub saw Trent look up and nod at Hap, then before he knew it, Cub felt Trent's hand on his shoulder. The heat from Trent's hand shocked him and his laughter disappeared.

Cub felt shaky as he grabbed his skateboard and pushed off down the street, Trent beside him. The laughter had left him feeling light, unweighted.

But *scared* was in there somewhere, too. Cub Tanner was downright scared. The Question fluttered against his neck.

Cub looked up into the dark sky as he continued skateboarding toward town. He could see a few stars twinkling between branches of the pines. He looked for the constellations Ursa Major and Ursa Minor, but it was hard to look for stars while he was going so fast, and those pines... He wished the sky were broader, that there weren't so many trees between himself and the stars.

All of a sudden he was in a different place on a different night, years before. When he was eight or nine, his dad had taken him on a camping trip far out to west Texas, where they'd camped on a broad, flat mesa. Much to Cub's delight, his mom had stayed at home with his toddler brother. It was just he and his dad.

That night the two of them lay down on the ground, side by side. Cub remembered resting his head on his father's arm, using it as a pillow. He remembered his father's smell, like the pine trees in their home in Dogwood, a strong smell of forests and earth. Like the smell that was still in his old army shirt. Using a flashlight as a pointer, his dad directed Cub's gaze toward the sky. He circled the planets—Jupiter, Venus, Saturn. Then he showed him the constellations. When he got to Ursa Major and Minor, he said, "Those are the Starbears, Cub. They watch over you."

Cub had reached up with both hands. The stars seemed so close. They rested right on the tips of his fingers. As he lay there beside his father, stars on his fingertips, he felt like he was glowing, as if the light from the stars were filling him up, like a river fills a lake—to the brim.

The bears beamed down at him, the little one following the bigger one as they circled the sky. Cub lowered his arms and closed his eyes. He was sure he could feel their warm breath on his neck, right beneath his chin, and there next to his father, bears above him, he felt completely and utterly safe.

"Hey, Tanner!" Trent's voice broke through the thick, humid air. Cub could hear him before he could see him. He glided down the sidewalk bordering the junior high.

"Trent?" Cub said, as he hopped off his skateboard and grabbed it.

"Over here, man." Cub looked under the parking lot light beside the back door of the school. There was movement. Then Trent, his black hair gleaming in the misty light, stepped out and grabbed Cub by the sleeve.

"Sorry I'm late," Cub whispered.

"No sweat, buddy." Trent patted Cub on the shoulder. "Let's fly." And with that the two headed toward Elizabeth's house, just a few blocks away.

The ground fog circled around them, hiding

them from the occasional streetlight, almost as if the air itself were a conspirator in their mission. Cub had never done anything like this before, never snuck out of his house without anyone knowing. He looked over at Trent, whose arms were swinging in a smooth rhythm with his feet, and Cub felt a kind of thrill move through his body. His heart raced as they cruised along.

They went quickly about their escapade, wrapping first Elizabeth's front yard with three rolls of toilet paper and then Shannon's next door. At each house they worked silently, tossing the rolls high into the trees and catching them softly as they streamed back to Earth. Their paper tails floated behind them and landed, white streamers in the arms of the branches.

When the boys were done, they walked across the street and admired their handiwork. The white wrapping glowed in the damp darkness.

"Hey, man. We are way too cool," Trent said.

Cub laughed. As he stood there, next to Trent, in the middle of the night with his family asleep miles away, he felt more than too cool. He felt awesome.

So when they got back to school, Cub wasn't

ready for it all to end. Just as Trent started to skate off toward his house, Cub yelled out, "Hey! Do you want to try something really great?"

"What?" Trent asked, dragging one foot on the concrete to slow himself down.

"Come on, I'll show you," Cub answered. Then he led Trent to the side of the building, behind the cafeteria, where a single cottonwood tree stood about two and a half feet from the wall.

"So?" Trent asked. "You want to show me a tree?"

"No," Cub replied. Then he added, "Watch." And with that he wedged himself with his feet between the tree and the wall, and using the branches as rungs, climbed onto the roof.

Cub had passed that cottonwood tree hundreds of times in the past three years, ever since he had been in the sixth grade at Dogwood Junior High. Only recently had he noticed how close it was to the edge of the building.

And now here he was! At least twenty feet up. He looked down and waved to Trent. "Come on!" he said.

Trent followed. Once he was up, both of them looked back over the edge. The fog that had encircled

them on the ground made a blanket below them. But there on the roof, the air was clearer, cooler.

"This is the best!" Trent said.

Cub couldn't stand still. He began to gallop over the flat tar surface, leaping over the aluminum vents that stuck up here and there. Trent followed. They held out their arms and ran in a huge circle. Faster and faster. Their feet barely skimmed the surface of the roof.

Cub stretched his arms wider and started spinning round and round. As he spun, one sleeve of his shirt slipped off his arm. He slowed down to grab it, but when he did, he got the sudden urge to take the shirt completely off. He slipped out of the other sleeve, and threw the shirt up into the air. It floated down like a cloud.

Cub looked over and saw Trent slip off his own shirt and throw it up, up against the dark sky. Without hesitation Cub pulled off his T-shirt, too. He shivered as the soft fingers of the air rubbed against his bare ribs, and he spun around again. Laughter rolled out of him as he spun, then picked up and threw his shirts into the sky again.

He was dizzy with laughing and spinning, and slowed down to catch his breath. He saw Trent stop, too. Even in the darkness, Cub could see Trent's smile.

"Are you thinking what I'm thinking?" Cub asked. Trent nodded. In the next moment they were both stepping out of their shoes. Off came socks, then blue jeans, then underwear—all of it flying into the air, the white underwear glowing against the sky, clothes falling in scatters against the roof.

Then Trent picked up his shirt and held it over his head like a cape and began to run in large circles around the edge of the roof. Cub grabbed his shirt and followed.

Around and around they flew, faster and faster, sometimes dangerously close to the edge. Once Cub looked over the side and saw only darkness. He knew the gray concrete of the parking lot was below him, beneath the blanket of fog, but he didn't feel scared at all. Right then he was a flier, with the night brushing against his bare skin and only the stars and maybe an owl and each other to say they were there. He ran and ran.

Cub felt he could run like this forever on the roof of the Dogwood Junior High cafeteria, but soon his side began to ache and he had to slow down. He sucked in air in big gulps. Trent walked up beside him, also breathing hard. Sweat poured down Cub's chest and arms. His bare feet were sticky from the tar surface.

Without saying anything, he walked over to where the rest of his clothes lay scattered. He knew he should get dressed. But when he looked over at Trent, he saw him stretch out his clothes on the roof and then lay down on top of them. So Cub did it, too. Above them there were stars, millions of them.

At last, Cub thought, *I've found a place to look for stars that isn't blocked out by pine trees.*

As if he were reading Cub's thoughts, Trent said, "Dude, I've never seen so many stars."

Cub wanted to say something back, but he was afraid that if he did, he'd have to say something sensible, like, "Man, we gotta get going." He wasn't ready for going yet.

Not yet, not with the air so clear and stars jumbling and tumbling so close to his skin. He raised his hands toward them, his fingers outstretched. How far away were they? A million miles? More?

Then Trent broke the silence. "We gotta bring our boards up here next time."

"Yeah," said Cub. And he started to laugh again,

and the laughter opened all the doors inside him and the silence slipped away. They began to talk about everything. Elizabeth Bryan and Shannon Perez, their classes, the Stardust Dance that was coming up in two weeks, who might be crowned King and Queen.

"Maybe it'll be you and Elizabeth," Cub ventured.

Trent shrugged. "Maybe."

Cub smiled at Trent's self-assured response. He looked at the stars. For a moment he felt completely perfect. He stared at the sky, the perfect sky, and he saw Ursa Major and Ursa Minor. There they were, just as his father had pointed them out all those years before. He didn't know why, but suddenly he had to tell Trent about the night on the mesa and the Starbears, and his father's shirt. The words came rolling out of him in a stream, bumping against one another, sliding out into the open. He stopped. He'd never meant to share that with anyone, but it was as if the words had a force of their own. Cub couldn't slow them down. And then just as quickly as they had come, they stopped. He turned his head and looked at Trent, whose face was turned toward him, staring.

Cub suddenly felt exposed. He took a deep breath and shut his eyes tight against Trent's stare. When he opened them back up, Trent was still staring. It was like that first time, just a few weeks before in Pre-Algebra. Cub felt himself being beamed up into those eyes. Those eyes. And then, without meaning to, he reached over and placed his finger on Trent's cheek. Immediately, he pulled it back. His fingertip was burning.

Trent yelled, "Oh my God!"

Cub shook his hand as if trying to cool it.

Trent stood up and pulled on his clothes. "I've got to go!" he cried.

Cub felt paralyzed as he watched Trent scramble across the roof and disappear over the edge. Then Cub panicked and ran to catch him, to tell him he had it all wrong. But all he could see was Trent's silhouette, rolling, rolling fast, until he vanished into the dark, dark night. And The Question dug its claws deep into Cub's shoulder.

Something like nausea, but worse, grabbed Cub at the base of his stomach, and he doubled over onto the tar surface of the roof, falling upon his knees and forearms. He lay there for a moment in a ball, his knees pulled tightly beneath his chin.

Then he rolled onto his back. When he looked up, the twinkling bears gleamed at him.

"I hate you!" he screamed. "I hate you!" He stood and picked up the army shirt. With all his might, he threw it at the stars. "You're supposed to look out for me!"

He didn't watch to see where the shirt fell. He didn't notice the damp air as it clung to his skin. He didn't feel the hot tears as they ran down his cheeks.

"What's wrong with me, anyway?" he sobbed. He looked below and knew that if he jumped off the edge now, he'd simply crash into the hard ground— he wouldn't fly at all, not even for a second.

The next few days were a blur. Cub avoided Trent as best he could, darted past him in the hallways, stayed behind him when the bell rang. Once he was sure that he'd heard Trent call out his name, but he pretended he hadn't. He asked Mrs. Burrows to move his desk to the opposite side of the room in Pre-Algebra. He found a different table to sit at during lunch. He stayed home after school instead of going out to skate. He certainly didn't plan to go to the Stardust Dance.

But his mother had signed up to be a chaperone.

"Look, Cub, if I'm going, you're going," she insisted.

So, just a few days later, he found himself at the Stardust Dance in the cafeteria of Dogwood Junior High School, with the other graduating eighth graders. His mother had won. He glanced at her, standing by the refreshment table with the chaperones. Her back was to him.

He hoped Trent wasn't there. He wasn't sure what he'd do if he saw him. He looked around. There was no corner or hall that he could duck into. He felt the cold blast of the air conditioner blow onto his face. He shivered. The Question tightened its grip.

From somewhere nearby, Shannon Perez sashayed up to him. "Let's dance," she said, and grabbed him by the elbow. Her hand was soft in his, and she smelled like vanilla ice cream. *I should feel lucky*, he thought as he watched her body begin to sway to the beat of the music.

He followed her onto the dance floor, the Rot Whilers, tattooed and pierced, playing. The music swept over him. It pounded through him, around him, up from the floor, through his feet. Shannon danced close, her vanilla ice-cream smell filling up his nostrils, her hands resting on his shoulders. She was lovely. Lovely enough to be a mermaid...or even the Stardust Queen.

Then he happened to glance past Shannon's dark hair to the decorations on the walls: large rolls of white butcher paper painted deep, deep blue, with stars shimmering everywhere. Against the blue background were two constellations in silver: Ursa Major and Ursa Minor. The Starbears.

And right beside them, against the wall—Trent Davis. Trent nodded and broke into a smile. The famous Trent Davis smile. He held up his forefinger and pointed toward the ceiling. Cub didn't understand at first. Then suddenly the message was clear, blazing in midair, like a comet.

He felt a shift in his whole body, as if he were being lifted off the floor. As if gravity had slipped away, disappeared, and every muscle, every tendon, every bone sought a higher elevation. His head began to spin, and he realized he was shivering, preparing for liftoff. It took every ounce of concentration he had to stay on the ground.

When the song was over, he excused himself from

Shannon, who gave him a puzzled look, and slipped past the chaperones and out the side door. Quickly he ran to the back of the building, wedged himself between the cottonwood tree and the wall, and shimmied to the top. He paused at the edge of the roof until his eyes adjusted fully to the darkness. Then he walked in a wide circle, his eyes scanning the surface.

There was nothing. Was this a trick Trent was pulling, some way of getting back at him? Cub felt his cheeks begin to burn. He clenched his fists and turned to go back down.

Then he saw it. Folded neatly and sitting next to an aluminum vent—his father's shirt. Cub reached down and picked it up. It was a little stiff and had an unfamiliar mustiness to it, but once he had both arms in the sleeves, he was sure he could again smell pine trees and forests and dark red earth. Cub started to button the shirt, but as he pulled it closed he noticed something in the pocket. He reached in and felt the cellophane. A Moon Pie.

And something else. A note.

He couldn't see it clearly in the darkness beneath the stars, and so he walked to the edge where a little light filtered up from the parking lot. There, in Trent's scrawling hand, the words: *For luck.*

So here he is alone on this May night, sitting on the roof, looking into the sky, waiting. He feels the music drift up through the ceiling, feels the great bears peering down at him, feels his father's arms hugging him through the old army shirt, feels the Moon Pie tucked into the pocket next to the note.

He thinks he might start laughing. Or crying. He's not sure which. Instead he takes a deep breath, closes his eyes, rests his head on his knees, and sighs. The cool air swirls around him, the new leaves in the cottonwood rustle softly. The Question whispers in his ear.

Only this time it's not digging into his shoulder. It's flying away. He realizes . . . he doesn't need to ask it anymore.

The Right Word

$\mathscr{B}$ecca Scott sits on the toilet in the last stall of the girls' bathroom, the pounding rhythm of the drums from the Stardust Dance down the hall driving right up through her body, matching her quick heartbeat. Her wet blue mascara and aqua eye shadow run down the side of her face.

She closes her eyes and imagines all her friends, dancing beneath the sparkly lights from the mirror-ball. It feels like they're on another planet, the Dogwood Junior High planet. And here she is in her own orbit, a thousand miles down the hall from all those dancers. People she knew just a few hours ago. She holds out her shaking hand and looks at it. *Would they know me now?* she wonders.

She looks at the smudged walls that surround her,

close her in like a turtle in a cardboard box. A school year's worth of graffiti jumps out at her: *Lacey + John 4-Ever. Dogwood is #1. Turn Your Heart to Jesus. Algebra Sux.*

The words pulse in front of her, in time to the driving drums: *Tommy gives great kisses. Monica is a slut. Go Lumberjacks. Carly loves Javier.* The tears stream down as she whispers each message. Then she comes to *Ty Charbonneau is sooooo GOOD,* and the walls begin to spin.

She reaches out and presses both hands against them. *Stop!* she almost cries out loud. That word: *GOOD.* It's such a small word. She's known how to spell it since the first grade.

She steadies herself and digs into her purse for a pen. She needs a marker, like the aqua-colored one she bought at Wal-Mart last week. Is it still there? No. Only her metal fingernail file.

She pulls it out and looks at it, the rough sides, the bright point, the tortoiseshell handle. She scrapes the file against the wall. Nothing. She presses a little harder. A slight scratch. She grips the metal blade between her first finger and thumb and pushes it into the beige enamel paint. A flake peels up, leaving a shiny, jagged line on the wall.

A small smile crosses her face.

This was Friday, wasn't it? Every Friday since first grade, there was a spelling test. Each Monday the list, each Friday the test. Tonight is the last Friday of the eighth grade. The Friday of the Stardust Dance. The Friday she'd been waiting for.

Tonight, *she* gets to make the list.

GOOD

Mamaw and Paps were good, there was no doubt about that. They could always make her laugh. "The world's glum enough without us addin' to it," Mamaw always said anytime Becca felt blue. "Yep," Paps would add. "No sense in wearing out your muscles with a frown when a smile feels better to your face."

They weren't at all like their daughter, her mother, who'd left Becca at the age of four, along with a trail of bad debts and an outstanding arrest warrant, left her on Mamaw and Paps's front porch—all for some guy who drove a motorcycle and rode her off down the main street of Dogwood without a backward glance.

Mamaw and Paps didn't make an issue of it. They just showed Becca right to her new bedroom, which used to be Mamaw's sewing room, and told her she was home.

Becca pauses and brushes the flakes of paint away, watches them drift to the floor and settle beside her foot, like tiny torn feathers from a colorless bird. She breathes in, exhales. The fingernail file feels warm in her palm. She grips it tightly and begins the next word.

FAIRYTALE

Is it one word or two? It doesn't matter. She was in the wrong one, anyway. In the right one, she would meet Ty and slip away with him, only for a few hours, slip out the bathroom window, just like a princess would slip out of a tower. In the right one, he'd carry her away to some enchanted place, maybe a jeweled castle, or a secret cove, or even a cozy gingerbread cottage in the forest—some wonderful place where they'd dance, the music swirling all around them, her new dress sparkling in the glimmery light. In the right one, she'd rest her head against his broad chest and he'd gently stroke her hair.

The plan was all so perfect. Becca remembered looking at the cafeteria clock and willing the hands to move faster. To hurry up until the appointed hour. Her heart had pounded. At last the time came and she'd quietly slipped off to the bathroom. No one would ever know except her best friend, Lindy, and Becca knew she would never tell.

She'd lifted the window and there he was. Pacing. He took her hand in his and briefly kissed her. In the fairy tale, she would have ridden with him in a carriage, but instead she rode on the seat beside him in his red Ford F-10 pickup truck. No matter. She felt beautiful as they drove through the night.

In the fairy tale, the Beast should have turned into a handsome prince as soon as the Beauty kissed him. Just like that—*poof!* One prince all spiffed up in a dashing cape, his eyes flashing, love just oozing out of him.

PRICE

What she paid for a kiss. In the fairy tale, she was supposed to get the Prince. But the small *n* was missing. How did it get away? What happened to happily ever after?

CHEAP

It's what they'll call her when they find out. No one will believe her. "Did you see what she was wearing?"

"What did she expect, sneaking out the bathroom window like that?" "Who's surprised, considering her mother?" They'll bring her mother into it, even though her mother has been gone for ten years. Becca knows they'll bring her up, can hear their words ringing through her ears, in perfect syncopation with the drums.

BEAUTY

Tyson D. Charbonneau. Hair the color of sand, eyes so brown they're nearly black. Almost as tall as Paps, over six feet, even though he's only eighteen. Star running back on the Dogwood High School varsity football team. Leading scorer on the basketball team.

Everyone in Dogwood thinks he's the cat's meow, as Mamaw would say. Seems like his name is in the *Dogwood Carrier* at least once a week. "Ty Charbonneau Puts Lumberjacks Ahead with Last-Minute Basket." "Charbonneau Named Most Valuable Player." "Mayor Declares Wednesday 'Ty Charbonneau Day.'"

Becca thinks the whole county is in love with Ty Charbonneau. She should know. Yes, she should.

SMITTEN

Rhymes with *kitten*. What Mamaw would call her if she knew. Ever since she'd met Ty last month at Hap's Gee-Rodge, where she and Lindy had stopped on their way home from school to buy some almond M&M's and a Dr. Pepper to split, Becca's been charmed. When Ty was offered a big football scholarship from Texas A&M University, she cut his picture out of the paper and pasted it into her scrapbook. She said his name to herself over and over, like a chant. But her feelings for Ty were bigger than *smitten*. Bigger than any single word could describe. Bigger than complete sentences, even. She thought they might swallow her whole if she wasn't careful.

Before tonight all she could talk about was Ty. She knew Lindy was sick of it. Ty this and Ty that, and "Isn't Ty cool?" and "Ty is so awesome." But she couldn't talk to Mamaw and Paps about him. With Ty being four years older than her, they'd never approve. Never.

It was Ty who'd told her that her eyes were aqua.

AQUA

Her Keds tennis shoes, her crop-top T-shirt that she'd found at the Saint Thomas Aquinas Thrift Store, the polish on her fingernails, the shimmery dress and strappy sandals she wore to the dance. Ever since that day when he told her, "Your eyes are aqua," everything had been aqua. She even wrote their names on her binder in aqua ink with her new marker. *Ty + Becca.* And she drew an aqua heart around them.

They won't print the names in the *Dogwood Carrier,* but everyone will know. They won't say she was wearing this new aqua dress. She's still wearing it, torn, in the bathroom stall—and she's shivering, even though the air is warm and the fingernail file in her hand burns the skin on her fingers.

BEAST

Who is the beast? Ever since she was small, she'd heard Paps tell the story about the panther, the one who roamed the farthest side of the piney woods, lurking, waiting. "His coat's the color of sand," he said, "and his eyes are so brown, they're nearly black. The thing about his eyes is that they'll draw you in if you're not careful. That's how powerful he is. He doesn't have to creep up on his prey. He waits for them to come to him."

PAINTER

What Paps calls a *panther*. He says the hunters used to cover these parts. "Every weekend they'd come to hunt the painters." His blue eyes blaze when he talks about it. According to Paps, they came and came until there was only one old painter left in the whole forest—a huge one, granddaddy to dozens of wildcats, now all gone.

"The hunters kept tryin' to get him, but each time they almost tracked him down, he dodged them 'til they all gave up." Paps pauses, scratches the loose skin on his elbow, looks out into the dark woods next to their small house.

Becca was there, in the dark woods. This very night. There, instead of at the Stardust Dance. She slipped out the bathroom window and let herself be led into the dark, dark woods, far away from the Dogwood Junior High cafeteria, with its dancers and drummer.

BONE OF TRUTH

What Mamaw says there isn't any of when it comes to the painter. "That's just an old wives' tale," she says. She pushes back a strand of gray hair, tucks it behind her ear. "There haven't been any painters in east Texas in half a century. Just wild hogs and raccoons."

Paps shakes his head, disagrees.

"Yep," he says. "On dark nights, when the air's still and hot, there's a good chance you'll see him out of the corner of your eye. Don't look directly at him, or he'll wrap his huge paws around you, hold your neck in his mouth, and drag you to his secret lair."

Does the bone crack if the truth is too heavy?

FAULT

Hers, for not listening to Lindy, who begged her not to go. Hers, for wearing aqua. Hers, for letting Bay out of the gate when she was eight—Paps's favorite redbone hound, silky ears and soft brown eyes, who howled at shooting stars.

Paps always told her, "That painter's always prowling, and if there's a child out late alone, in the forest, he'll take it as his own and never bring it back." He pauses. "He'll do the same with the hounds."

She can hear Paps chewing on his Copenhagen tobacco. She knows the next part of the story, and it makes the hairs stand up on her arms. "Only some do come back. Like Bay."

PIECES

When Bay came back, he was torn up, front leg dragging on the ground, useless, a huge flap of skin on his shoulder peeled back. It was the only time she'd ever seen Paps cry. If she could, she'd put all the pieces back in Bay's shoulder. She'd lock the gate.

And if she could, she'd go back and stay at the Stardust Dance. She'd dance through the night, beneath the cardboard moons and cutout stars. She'd hold her head back and laugh with Lindy and her other friends. She'd move to the beat of those drums.

DON'T

Don't let your children out at night. Keep them safe from the terrible painter. Tuck them in and say your prayers. Don't let them slip out the bathroom window at the Stardust Dance.

PROOF

"Don't you love me, Becca?" he had asked. They'd pulled off the main highway onto a dirt logging road. The headlights from the truck were penned in by the nearby trees. It felt as if they were driving through a pine tunnel, right into the forest's heart. When they finally stopped, Ty turned off the engine and walked around to her side. As he opened the door, the light from the cab illuminated his eyes. She looked directly into them and felt her breath catch. Such eyes.

He helped her out of the truck and led her to a small clearing a few feet away from the road. He spread a raggedy blanket on the soft ground, pulled her down beside him, and put his heavy arm around her shoulders, pressed his lips against her neck.

Did she love him? Of course she loved him. His sandy-colored hair, those dark brown eyes. The way he smelled, like soap and cigarettes and something else she couldn't name. Something like the resin from the pine trees, like the pitch beneath the loose bark, something thick and dark.

She felt wrapped in the smell of him. Did she love him?

"Prove it," he said. Then he lunged.

And there it was—the bruise on her shoulder, the cut on her cheek, her shimmery hose all torn and ragged. Like Bay's shoulder. Proof.

ALL RIGHT

It wasn't. Paps knew. Mamaw was wrong. The Beast was out there. Terrible. Waiting.

STOP

She wants to. Her fingers ache from the carving. But she's not quite done. She remembered yelling, "Stop!!!" at the top of her lungs, and her voice had come right back to her, bounced off the cold stars and witnessing trees. "Stop!! Please, please stop!" But the stars, the trees, Ty—none of them heard her.

And he didn't stop. He didn't.

Now she sucks in her breath. Flakes of paint drift to the tile floor. She thinks she can hear them when they land.

ASSAULT

It's what they'll call it in the newspaper *if* she reports it, but she knows it's too soft a word, the short vowels, the silky consonants. Even the *t* at the end barely rests atop the tip of her tongue. The wrong word. She scratches it out. The drummer down the hall picks up the pace, the rhythm gains speed.

Faster, faster. The list is almost done. Almost. Sweat trickles down her neck, down the back of her dress, and between her breasts. She thinks she might burst into flames. First letter—R. Second letter—A. Third letter—P. Fourth letter—E. The right word.

THE END

Suddenly, the drummer stops. The band must be taking a break. In a moment, she knows, the door to the bathroom will open and other girls will walk in, full of talk and laughter. They'll check their lipstick, comb their hair, adjust their strapless bras. Lindy will probably come in to see if she's returned. Becca takes off her aqua sandals so Lindy won't know it's her if she looks beneath the door of the stall. She slips her fingernail file back into her purse. The other girls will knock, wanting in, but she'll stay there until the dance is over and she can run to the parking lot. Run to Mamaw and Paps. Run, run, as fast as she can.

But first she rubs her fingers across the letters. Then she slumps forward in the tiny stall and rests her head against the cold metal door. Beside her the fresh words glow in the dim fluorescent light, like the shooting stars Bay once howled at. She checks the list again—each word, each letter. It's an easy list. She's good at spelling. She could win any spelling bee. She could be the queen. The Queen Bee. The Stardust Queen Bee. Then she'd snap her wings and make it all go away.

Kissing Tennessee

The answer wasn't clear at all to Peggy Lee Dixon, floating along the way she was, as if she were on a big, puffy cloud. But if a couple of birds flew by, one of them might look back over her shiny black wing and say, "Hey, did you see that girl over there? What's she doing up here in our sky?"

And the other one would say, "Leave her be, sister. That there is Peggy Lee Dixon, and all she's doin' is floatin'. No harm in floatin', is there?"

Then the first one would say, "But why's she floatin'?"

"'Cause Tennessee Jones finally passed the kiss test, that's why."

"The 'kiss test'! What in blue blazes is that?" By now the first bird would be gettin' agitated.

"Silly goose," bird number two would say. "That's when there's only one kiss in the whole movie, but that one kiss is worth the price of admission."

It's not the first time he's kissed her.

No, the original kiss was in the first grade. There she was in her favorite pink Wrangler jeans and her new pink sweater that her grandmother had given her for Christmas, leaning up against the brick wall next to the door of the first-grade wing at Dogwood Elementary School, just standing there, pink, waiting for the bell to ring. Two or three other first graders were standing there with her, but not Tennessee.

He was out on the playground with a big group of other kids.

So there she was, leaning against the wall, when all of a sudden Tennessee shot from the playground crowd like a meteor, his blond hair blazing in the sun, his blue-jeans jacket streaming behind him. Faster than the speed of light, he blew by her, paused only long enough to kiss her right on the mouth, then zoomed back into orbit.

"Tennessee Jones!" Peggy Lee yelled. "I'm telling!" And she did, too.

That particular kiss earned Tennessee a trip to the office, where Mr. Duncan, the principal, told him in

no uncertain terms that kissing on school property was not allowed.

Tennessee. Now there's a name for you. His mama named him that on account of their last name being so regular. "With a plain vanilla name like Jones, you gotta have a first name that's special," she'd said. Tennessee, almost the exact same age as Peggy Lee and whose yard shares a fence with hers, who comes in and out of the Dixons' back door a million times a day. What a name.

Peggy Lee. She was named after an old singer her daddy thinks was the best thing this side of the Mississippi (and maybe the other side, too). Her daddy is just wild about this one song she sings. He knows all the words to it, and when Peggy Lee was really little, he used to pick her up in his arms, take her outside on the porch, and sing that song over and over. "Is That All There Is?"

Peggy Lee loved the song then, but now that she's thirteen, almost fourteen, it drives her crazy when her daddy starts singing it, because as soon as he does, it gets stuck in her head and she can't get it out. It just keeps playing over and over, like a scene from a movie sometimes does. And it's such a hard song to figure out. Is it happy? Is it sad? Happy? Sad? It seems all jumbled up.

The next time Tennessee kissed Peggy Lee, it was not on school property. It was at the Dogwood North Little League Park.

When they'd both been in the fourth grade, they'd played on the same baseball team, the Cardinals. Those Cardinals made it all the way to the district playoffs. At the end of the championship game, they were behind by one run, 6–7, against the Lufkin Bearcats. It was the bottom of the ninth and the Cardinals were up to bat with two outs already. They had one runner on third base, and it was Peggy Lee's turn to bat.

None of the other boys on the team believed that she could hit against the Lufkin pitcher. But Tennessee yelled from the dugout, "Come on, Peggy Lee!"

That's one thing about Peggy Lee and Tennessee, they've always been there for each other. When Tennessee fell out of his tree house and broke his arm, Peggy Lee visited him at home every afternoon after school for the three whole days he was absent.

She brought his homework to him and notes from the other kids, and told him all the jokes she could think up to make him feel better.

When Peggy Lee couldn't quite figure out how to do the multiplication tables, Tennessee showed her how to line up the numbers in columns and then look at them like pairs. He said it so that everything made perfect sense. Even today Peggy Lee knows her multiplication tables backward and forward because of that.

When Bodger, Tennessee's old dog, died one winter, Peggy Lee used her daddy's shovel to dig a hole in the backyard to bury him while Tennessee sat on the ground, cradling Bodger in his arms and crying. Then she sat next to Tennessee and cried and cried right along with him. And she never told anyone about Tennessee crying, either, not a single person.

So when it was Peggy Lee's turn to bat at the district playoffs, when everyone else thought they'd lose for sure because it was her, Peggy Lee, at bat, there was Tennessee yelling, "Come on, Peggy Lee! You can do it!"

And she did. When the pitcher threw the ball, she could see it heading straight for her swing, see it coming directly at the sweet spot on her bat, see it connect with the aluminum, leather against metal.

Pow! The ball went deep into left field, way behind the Bearcats' fielder, giving the runner on third base time to score—and Peggy Lee, too. Everyone on the bench poured out onto the field. They were all hugging and jumping and giving high fives. Cardinals everywhere.

And smack in the middle of all the commotion, Tennessee looked right at Peggy Lee and planted one right on her mouth. Then he just started jumping up and down with the rest of them, like it never happened.

Later, while they were eating their complimentary snow cones, Peggy Lee said, "Why'd you do that?"

"Do what?" he asked, licking the red syrup that was running down the outside of his paper snow-cone cup and across the back of his hand.

"You know," she said, "kiss me like that."

He looked at her in total amazement. "Kiss you?" Then he leaned his head back and spit red ice straight up toward the stadium light. It glittered in the burning light.

———

But all of that was before tonight at the Stardust Dance. Tennessee's daddy had dropped them off in front of the cafeteria right at eight o'clock, just as the band was beginning to play. When they'd walked in, the place was all sparkly. There was glitter everywhere, sprinkled on the table by the punch bowl and cookies, sprinkled on the floor, glued onto the decorations. It was even tucked into the napkins, so that when you picked one up, glitter floated through the air.

It was wonderful—the glitter, the music, all their friends dancing and talking. Pretty soon they were dancing, too. Peggy Lee with J. T. Sims and Tennessee with Tessie Adams. Peggy Lee didn't only dance with J. T., either. Nope. And Tennessee, he didn't only dance with Tessie. Peggy Lee saw him dancing with Julia Marsh and Patty Henderson, too.

The whole evening was filled with laughing and dancing and glitter. But especially dancing. And now it was almost over. Only a few dances left.

Peggy Lee was just getting ready to grab J. T.'s hand and pull him out onto the floor, when there was Tennessee, right in front of her, just like those times in first grade and at the Little League park.

"Come on, Peggy Lee. This one's for me." And he wrapped his arms around her and pulled her close. All their lives they had been together, their houses backing up to each other. All their almost fourteen years they had been going in and out of each other's back doors without even knocking. Ever since they could remember, it had been Peggy Lee and Tennessee.

And in all that time, Peggy Lee didn't remember ever being so close to him as right then in the school cafeteria.

That's when she noticed how green his eyes were, and how tall he suddenly seemed to be, and how nice he smelled—like the spiced tea his mama made on cold afternoons when they came home from school to do their homework together. Like oranges and cinnamon and cloves. Like that.

She closed her eyes and took a deep breath, and when she opened them, the whole room was filled with glitter. Glitter floating all around them. Right then the only place in the world she wanted to be was up close to Tennessee.

"I'm gonna get this right," he said. And as the band began to play the first chorus of an old Aerosmith song, he leaned down and kissed her. Just like that. Kissed her right on the mouth, right there in the Dogwood Junior High cafeteria that was all filled up with glitter.

Flash! She opened her eyes just in time to see Sky Williams take their picture.

And that's when the floating had started. The cafeteria floor just fell away beneath her feet. And even though Tennessee is holding her hand, she's still way up off the ground, like one of those helium balloons, floating up there with the clouds and the comets and the birds.

Later, when she gets back home, that song of her daddy's will keep on playing over and over in her head. "Is That All There Is?" Later she'll feel that way, happy and sad all jumbled up together.

But right now, her head on Tennessee's shoulder, the music swirling around them, one thing's for certain. That kiss? That single kiss? It was worth the price of admission.

The Notes Between the Notes

It was just about time for the very last dance. The candles were almost completely burned out, except for a few that were barely flickering in their blue glass containers; the chaperones and teachers were getting the brooms out of the closets; the punch bowl was empty. It was almost done. Just a few moments left before the lights came back on and everything would go back to being the same.

And still, Carrie Marie Jorgensen and Mason Hatfield hadn't asked each other to dance.

Who would ever have thought that Carrie Marie Jorgensen—straight-A student; president of the student council; head of the Junior National Honor Society; lover of Beethoven, Bach, Emily Dickinson, and any other composer or poet who wrote prior to the twentieth century; who never ever never would have dreamed of turning in a late assignment; who planned to attend The Juilliard School on a scholarship when she graduated from high school, something she'd known ever since she became first-chair violinist of the Dogwood Junior High Orchestra in the sixth grade, as well as junior concert mistress in the Piney Woods Symphony—would fall so hard for Mason Hatfield?

Who would ever have thought that Mason Hatfield—average student; not-so-secret writer of limericks and puns on bathroom walls; owner of three identical black Pearl Jam T-shirts (one of which he wore every day over his baggy silverTab Levi's that threatened to drop below his knees if he broke into a slight jog); rider of a Dyno BMX bike that he could send flying over small hills with himself on the seat but that also kept his elbows in a perpetual state of raw skin from hitting the hard dirt from time to time; who had absolutely no idea when most of his assignments were due but usually managed to turn them in anyway in some form or another; who didn't have a clue about where he might go to college, or if he even would; but who also played in the

Dogwood Junior High Orchestra, where he was first chair by default because he was the only double bass player in the entire orchestra, but that didn't matter because he loved playing the bass, loved it so much he named his bass Pal on the first day of sixth grade, when Mr. White, the orchestra teacher, checked it out to him, loved the rich mellow way it sang to him, loved it even more than he loved his bike or Pearl Jam or his baggy jeans—would have fallen so hard for Carrie Marie Jorgensen?

Carrie, perfectly neat, with her curly brown hair and freckles, her hazel eyes.

Mason, perfectly messy, with his skinned elbows.

Why couldn't one of them ask the other to dance?

It was because there was a problem that they didn't know how to solve: Neither was certain of the way the other one felt. It was, after all, such an unlikely matchup. They were so surprised by their feelings, they hadn't told a soul. So no one knew. Not even each other.

And one dance was all that was left.

Carrie could hardly believe she felt so strongly about Mason Hatfield. Ever since she had been a very little girl, she'd been fairly certain that the type of guy she would fall for would resemble the Prince Charmings who showed up in all her old picture books.

In fact, in her diary she had written a secret list of the qualities that she expected in a beau: *tall, dark,* and *handsome* were at the top.

Mason was tall, but he had sort of greasy blond hair that he wore pulled back in a ponytail (and of course the ponytail was not supposed to be on the boy; it was supposed to be on the white horse that Prince Charming rode), and she wouldn't exactly call him *handsome.* Not Mason. He wasn't unattractive, he was sort of plain, but his blue eyes did sparkle, especially when he played Pal. Carrie knew this because from her first-chair seat in the orchestra, she sometimes glanced around her black music stand to catch a glimpse of Mason there next to his bass, caressing the strings with his bow. It took her breath away.

Oh, if he would only ask her to dance!

Brilliant was also on Carrie's list, and Mason certainly didn't fit that category—or at least if he did, he didn't show it. She knew he was something of a slouch when it came to grades, but still she was appalled when she heard he made a C in Science.

All of her friends would have died if they found themselves that low on the grading scale. But Mason didn't seem to mind at all. In fact, he seemed overjoyed when he didn't get an even lower grade from Mrs. Wassell, the science teacher, especially considering the stupid project he'd turned in for the eighth-grade science fair—a lame attempt to show that a bicycle would cover more miles in less time with more air in the tires. Carrie wanted to say "Duh" when he presented it in class. But she didn't.

Because even though the project was pretty dumb, she had to laugh when he performed it in the form of a twelve-bar blues song, accompanying himself on Pal.

> *"Oh-oh-oh, you'll go so slow-oh-oh.*
> *You got to fill those tires with air,*
> *Or you won't hardly,*
> *You won't barely,*
> *You won't never get past anywhere."*

Carrie had never even heard a twelve-bar blues progression before that. It wasn't anything like Mozart.

She was sure the last dance wasn't going to be Mozart, either. Nor would it be the blues. It would probably be a slow number, one that repeated the word *love* several times, one that would let her get close enough to him to see his blue eyes. Close enough to rest her hand on his shoulder. Close enough to... Her thoughts were racing now.

She made a wish—*Please, oh please, let me be chosen Stardust Queen and Mason be chosen King. That way we'll have to dance.* The wish shocked her. Until that very moment, Carrie had thought the whole Queen and King business was silly and immature. But these were desperate times.

She could see Mason across the room with his buddies, Mike Adams and Janie Powell. His back was to her. What if she just walked over and tapped him on the shoulder? Would he even want to dance with her? What if he turned her down?

On Carrie's Prince Charming list, she had also written *romantic.* Mason Hatfield romantic? No way. In fact, one of the few times he had ever spoken directly to her, all he'd talked about were his bike jumps and skinned elbows, which he reported at breakneck speed, as if he had to get the story told and get away from her as quickly as possible. It was hard for Carrie not to be somewhat disgusted by the skinned elbows, and she looked away when he started to show her his scabs.

But she still liked the telling of his stories, the

being directly across from him so that she could see his blue eyes flashing, the way he used his skinny arms and broad hands to show how he held on to the handlebars when he went over a jump, the funny *errrrttt* and *vrrooom* sounds he made to illustrate how he braked and how he scooted across the course, the way he smelled like Irish Spring soap and Trident cinnamon gum mixed together.

Carrie sighed. The candles burned lower.

About the only quality that Mason actually met on Carrie's list was *Must like music.* But Carrie was glad that she had never specified what kind of music Prince Charming had to like, because in the case of Mason, she didn't think they liked any of the same music at all, even though they both played in the orchestra and got to take the solos, since they were both first chairs.

Carrie had to admit that Mason did play his bass well. But he **rar**ely played what was written on the page, which was a source of some consternation to Mr. White, and was for a long time an irritation to Carrie, who liked a more orderly approach to music.

"I like to figure out what's between the notes," Mason had told her one day when she asked him in a rather snippy way why he couldn't play the piece as it was written. "It's not that I can't," he'd said, his blue eyes looking directly at her, "it's that there are so many more interesting notes in between." Then, with his long skinny arms, he reached toward her, softly popped her on the head with his sheet music folder, and with a loud *"vrrroom,"* he walked around her and out of the music room.

That had been the moment when Mason Hatfield with his skinny arms and bass named Pal transformed—baggy jeans and all—smack into Prince Charming.

Carrie Marie Jorgensen came from another planet as far as Mason Hatfield was concerned. A planet of straight A's and dental floss and plans for the future and well-thought-out science projects. But ever since that moment in the music room—when he had told her about the notes between the notes and looked directly into her hazel eyes, which reminded him of the pine trees outside the window of his room, and seemed to understand completely what he was saying even though he wasn't sure he understood it himself—he hadn't been able to think of anything except Carrie Marie Jorgensen.

And now the last dance was almost here.

The night had slipped away without even so much as a word between them. Mason grimaced. That was part of the problem. Lately, whenever he was around Carrie, he said the stupidest things. It was like his mouth disconnected from his brain and just spouted out things that had been lodged in his cheeks or maybe even his nose, just waiting for a chance to say something dumber than dumb to one of the smartest girls in Dogwood, maybe one of the smartest girls in the world.

All that junk about riding his bike. Like she could care? One day he'd even told her all about his skinned elbow and had shown her the scabs that he had been picking at for hours. When he looked at the disgust on her face, all he could think of was getting away from her as fast as he could. How stupid could you get? Scabs?

He suddenly felt all of his Ban Ultra Dry Roll-On roll on down the sides of his rib cage and soak into the waistband of his Joe Boxer boxer shorts. He grabbed the top of his Levi's and bolted through the doors.

But as soon as he was out of her sight, he wanted to be back in it. Looking at her curly hair. Looking for the dimple that appeared whenever she smiled. Talking again about the in-between notes.

He wanted to drift away on the violin solo that she played in the Mozart piece they were working on in orchestra, wanted to hook into her concentration. Wanted to be wherever she was.

What was it with this girl?

And why couldn't he force himself to ask her to dance? His scabs were healed. He had on his cleanest Pearl Jam T-shirt. His mother had made him wear a belt, so his pants wouldn't hobble him at the knees while he danced. He had even washed his hair twice and used conditioner. And earlier in the evening he had slipped into the bathroom and put on a second coating of Ban Ultra Dry.

The thing was, he loved to dance. In fact, he had danced to almost every song. Danced with his old buddy Tawny Raymond. Danced with Peggy Lee Dixon. With Mary Sarah Luther. With Shannon Perez. None of them had said no. Why would Carrie?

And he had seen her dance, too. Seen her float across the floor. Seen her smile at Sky Williams. Seen her hug Cub Tanner. Seen her hold hands with Mack Sanders while he led her to the dance floor.

Would she smile at *him*? Would she give *him* a hug? Would she hold his hand if he asked? The last dance was always a slow one. Would she put her head against his pounding chest? Could he rest his face in her curly hair, which he was sure smelled like roses or mint or maybe pine trees?

Could he find the notes between the notes?

The drummer in the band was counting.... "A one, a two, a one-two-three-four..."

These Shoes

"*W*ear these," your mama, Caledonia, whispers, handing you maybe the ugliest pair of shoes in Dogwood County. Make that on the planet.

These shoes are so ugly they make your eyes water. Faded, faded black, no shine at all, not any, with ragged thin straps that buckle around your ankles. Even worse, they have big red rhinestone bows on the toes that look like something Toto chewed off Dorothy's ruby slippers and your mother stitched on crooked. A few of the rhinestones are missing, too, like maybe Toto shook the bows too hard.

How can you be crowned Stardust Queen with these things on your feet? No queen would be caught dead with these on, that's for certain.

You're about to say, "Unh-uhh, no way am I

gonna wear these ugly things. Makes my feet hurt just lookin' at them." But Caledonia speaks first.

"Tawny, you can dance all night in these," she says. You've never heard Caledonia speak in such a faraway voice like that, like she wasn't even in the room, like she was drifting maybe. And even though you're several inches taller than her, your eyes meet as if you weren't taller at all.

She says it again. "You can dance all night."

And you think, *Like I might die all night.* You've waited for this dance all year, the Stardust Dance. And you know you've got a slender chance of being chosen Queen. It's slender, but it's there, the chance.

And you want it. You want that chance.

Just like you want other chances. A chance to be someone who doesn't live in the East Pine Trailer Park, for starters. A chance to live in a real house, with a real garage on the side and a real yard for your little dog, Brodie. Even a chance to get a tattoo. Not a big one, like the dragon Patti Henderson had tattooed all the way up her calf. No, not like that. You'd get a small one, maybe a tattoo of hearts all the way around your ankle, red and blue hearts, little tiny ones that look like teardrops.

Hearts. Hearts are like your logo. You draw them all the time. While you're supposed to be listening to your English teacher, Mrs. Dove. While you're talking on the phone. While you're doing your homework. You love the shape of them, the idea of them, the way they look on paper.

They'd look better on skin, you think. A tattoo bracelet of hearts. That's what you'd get if Caledonia weren't your mother.

Then you'd go to the dance without shoes, especially without the ones Caledonia has shoved under your nose. These ugly shoes with the rhinestone bows.

Your grandmother, Cleo, has bought you a brand-new dress to wear. It's a soft red, not fire-engine red or screaming red but a kind of crimson that looks soft.

It's made of silky crepe, sleeveless, with a pearl neck and bodice that hugs you just so down to your waist. You've never had a dress you like so much. The skirt comes just above your knees and flares out when you walk. When you first put the dress on right after dinner, you stood in front of the mirror in Caledonia's room and in your stocking feet you twirled around, watched the skirt float above your hips. You spun and spun. And you thought about how you would go gliding out onto the floor at the Stardust Dance.

But Cleo didn't think about shoes to go with it. And you didn't realize that you'd outgrown the patent leather pumps she'd bought you at Christmas. So here you are, in this wonderful dress, with no shoes.

Your chance for queendom is dashed. Instead, someone else will probably be chosen Queen. Someone like Peggy Lee Dixon or Carrie Marie Jorgensen.

Seemed like you had lots of chances before you moved here to the East Pine Trailer Park, before Caledonia took on that second job at the Dogwood County Hospital as an admissions clerk in the evenings, in addition to her regular job as a receptionist during the day for the Pine Forest Timber Company. Before your daddy moved away. Left you and Caledonia one sunny morning. There you both were, you and Caledonia, sitting at the breakfast table, sun pouring in through the window. You were eating a bowl of Froot Loops and Caledonia was slicing a peach and in walked your daddy with his suitcase.

He stood in front of the window, and for a moment you thought he was a cloud that was going to rain any second, standing there blocking the sun the way he was.

Instead, he pursed his lips and looked at Caledonia. "I'm outta here," he said. Then he was gone and the sun filled up the room again. You wanted Caledonia to run after him. But she just sat there. So it was you who ran. You dropped your spoon into the Froot Loops and ran out the kitchen door, down the steps, out to the driveway, where he was getting into his blue Ford Taurus, the one he'd bought from his boss, Mr. Evans, at the Dogwood Hardware Store.

You ran out there in your Little Mermaid pajamas, Froot Loops stuck to the front of them.

But your daddy held his hand up like a crossing guard. *Stop.* And so you did. Then you looked over your shoulder, because you just knew that Caledonia would come get him. But she didn't. She didn't even leave the kitchen table.

That was six years ago. And last anyone heard, he was living in Florida in a condominium on the beach.

After that you moved to the East Pine Trailer Park because your grandmother Cleo is there, and with Caledonia working so much, Cleo can help keep an eye on you. But that's the trouble, there are too many eyes on you, two of which are looking at you right now. Caledonia's eyes, deep brown like yours. And at the moment, so dreamy.

You don't really know what to say. She works so hard and you know she's working because she wants you to attend college. Caledonia never went to college. Cleo didn't, either. But you? You want to go more than anything. The University of Houston, that's where you want to be someday—maybe more than you want to be Queen—but you're afraid you don't have the brains to get in. Since when did anyone in the East Pine Trailer Park have enough brains to get into college?

If only your daddy were here. Then maybe it wouldn't matter if you had brains, because he'd find a way for you to get to college no matter what. But your daddy is far away in Florida and he hasn't even written you a letter since that day he held up his hand, not even a birthday card or a Christmas card or a postcard. All because Caledonia didn't tell him to stop, didn't follow him out to the driveway

and make him take the key out of his blue Ford Taurus.

Does he even know you're living in the East Pine Trailer Park, where the roads aren't even asphalt but instead are just dirt, red dirt that seeps into everything including the furniture, the walls, your hair, your skin, the backs of your hands? Does he know you're taller than your mother now? Does he know you can't remember the color of his eyes?

And what you really want to do is pitch a fit because it's all so unfair. If you had a different mother than Caledonia, everything would be different. Your father would not have left you in your Little Mermaid pajamas with Froot Loops on them. You wouldn't live in the smallest trailer in the East Pine Trailer Park, where you're ashamed to bring your friends because all of them—except Manny Folkes, who lives two trailers over but who doesn't count because he's so short—live in regular houses with garages and real wood paneling on the living room walls.

Then you wouldn't get called trailer trash whenever you step onto the school bus. "Trailer trash." You hear it just beneath the skin, just below the sound level. You know it's been said only loud enough for you to hear. Loud enough to hear but not loud enough for you to know who said it. There it hangs above the green vinyl seats in the air of the school bus, like a bubble, moving along with you and the rest of the kids at thirty miles per hour all the way to school.

You hate living there with Caledonia. Caledonia who doesn't know anything.

All you two do is argue anymore. Used to be Caledonia could make you laugh until your sides ached and tears ran down your face, like when you were little and Caledonia pretended to be Booger Mama, and she'd get down on her hands and knees and start crawling toward you and you'd see her coming and you'd scream at the top of your lungs and laugh so hard and she'd be singing in a low voice, "Here comes Booger Mama. Gonna tickle, tickle, tickle." Then she'd grab you and tickle you and finally hug you so tight and sing "You Are My Sunshine" over and over and over, kissing you and singing and hugging you at the same time.

And you remember her breath when she kissed you, how it always smelled like the chamomile tea she drinks in the evening before bed.

Oh sure, she rubs you on the back once in a while, or she pushes your hair out of your face, but you'd rather she didn't do that, so when she does you toss your head or try to move her hand away.

And now here she is, handing you these ugly faded shoes with the ruby bows and the thin straps. And you don't really want to touch them. You want to move them away, too. You're about to tell her that you can't go to the dance with those shoes. That you'll be called trailer trash for sure. And you don't think you can stand hearing it even one more time. But it's Caledonia that makes you stop.

She's looking down at the pair of shoes and you notice her face, how soft it is, pale almost, but she seems to be glowing. Glowing. Like there's a light inside her. Like she has a halo or something. Like she knows something you don't know.

"Be brave," she says. And suddenly you know she's setting you free, free to make up your own steps. Then, from out of nowhere, she adds, "I'm sure he still loves you," even though you haven't said a word. How does she know that? How does anyone know what another person thinks? Like, how does Caledonia think she knows that you want to wear these ugly shoes she's handing you? Which you don't. And you feel trapped. What other shoes are you going to wear? The only other pair in your closet are your orange Converse high-tops, which you love, love, love, but even you know they won't go with your silky red dress.

"You can dance all night in these," Caledonia says again, and there's a kind of insistence in her voice that makes you sigh and take the shoes in your hand. You look at them and wonder, *Will they get me home if I click my heels together three times?*

Home. Where is that? In the house you used to live in, where sunlight splashed across the kitchen table? In a condominium in Florida? In your new red dress here in the East Pine Trailer Park, with Cleo and Caledonia?

You wait for her to say something else, something more. But there is no further explanation. That is all.

So you slip them on, fasten the buckles. You're a little surprised that they fit, because Caledonia is smaller than you. But they slide right on as if they'd been custom ordered from Dillard's department store or even that fancy place in Houston, Neiman Marcus. You look down at them and you can't even see the missing rubies.

When you stand up again, Caledonia grabs your hands and before you know it, she's holding you and the two of you are dancing together right there in the living room. *One, two, three. One, two, three.* You're waltzing around the coffee table, singing "You Are My Sunshine" together, which isn't even a waltz, sashaying all around that room. Caledonia is laughing. You are, too. The air is filled with chamomile.

Later, when Caledonia drops you off at school, you wave good-bye to her and she shouts out, "Dance one for me!"

And once inside, you're surprised that no one says anything at all about the shoes, not a word, and you begin to wonder if maybe they're magic or invisible or something, but then you decide that probably no one notices them because your red dress fills up their eyes.

You dance and dance. And the dancing is so good, it doesn't matter that you aren't chosen Stardust Queen. All you want to do is dance. You dance with

Tennessee Jones, who is one of the few boys who is taller than you. You dance with Mason Hatfield, who doesn't even notice your dress, much less your shoes. And you dance with Manny Folkes, who doesn't really count because he's so short.

A splash of light catches your eye. Sky Williams takes your picture as you spin across the floor, and suddenly everything counts: Manny Folkes, the dress, your father in Florida, the cards he never writes, tattooed hearts, Cleo, going to the University of Houston, Caledonia, especially Caledonia, with her two jobs. All of it counts. Then you remember the last thing Caledonia said to you, "Dance one for me!"

And so when the band begins playing the last song, you look down at the shoes and smile. You spin by the cafeteria windows, where you can see your reflection shining back at you on the panes of glass, so light, so lovely, so free.

All of you are there. Mirrored on the dark panes. Lucy White with Tim Hernandez. Mary Sarah Luther, prettier than you remember. Tennessee Jones, holding Peggy Lee Dixon's hand. Cub Tanner and his best friend, Trent Davis, with Shannon Perez and Elizabeth

Bryan. Brooke Patterson and Russ Mills. Even Mason Hatfield and Carrie Marie Jorgensen. Sky Williams, snapping pictures for the yearbook. All of you, in this one night, in this one place...together.

Shining.

# Midnight

The night janitor unlocks the door—
she's glad for the work,
her favorite night of the year.

The room is warm
with leftover sweat.
Bodies leaned together, hands held
behind the backs of invisible chaperones—
now all gone.
Their voices
hang in whispers.

She takes a deep breath, and oh,
the sweet scent of endings:
the glitter, the spilled punch, the cookie
crumbs...
a pause and their spent laughter soaks
into the dusty floor,
shed tears slip between the cracks,
secret stars beneath her leather shoes.

In a moment
she'll rub it all in with her
heavy mop,
wax it into the linoleum tiles—

keep it safe, unseen until next May
when the drummer will come in early,
set up his equipment, and leave.

Can't we see? The cymbals will shimmer
all alone,
the first miracle
on such a night as this.

Acknowledgments

Not one of these stories happened in isolation. Each and every one benefited from the generous and loving attention paid to it by a host of readers. In particular I want to thank Debbie Leland, Donna Cooner, Robert Fowler, Jean and Fred Heath, Anne Bustard, Meredith Charpentier, Toni King, David Rosen, Jo Spiller, Pat Childress, and Joy Hein. Thanks to Paul Robertson of the Texas Parks and Wildlife Department for assuring me that there was at least one verifiable "painter" in east Texas. A warm hug goes to Elizabeth Neeld, who provided her cabin in Soddy Daisy, Tennessee, for the time it took to write the early drafts of "Rachel's Sister."

From the start this book was "believed in" by my

agent, Marilyn Marlow, who gave me the encouragement I needed to complete it. Her faith in me and these stories stands as a great gift. Good fortune smiled when my editor, Allyn Johnston, at Harcourt, bought the manuscript and brought her belief and support to the mix. Thanks also to her assistant, Karrie Oswald, who knew just the right questions to ask, and to Robin Cruise, for her attention and tenacity in the unforgiving task of copyediting.

In the eleventh hour Anne Langdon and her students at College Station Junior High "field-tested" the stories. I'm indebted to them for their care and honesty.

Not a word would ever get written if it weren't for the ongoing support of my incredible husband, Ken, and my two sweet sons, Jacob and Cooper.

Finally, I send my deepest gratitude to my late teacher, Venkatesh Kulkarni, who I know is still guiding me.